The Sound of Rain

Hana Ferguson

For Tanner; thank you for teaching me that being different is beautiful.

Love, Hana

THE SOUND OF RAIN

HANA FERGUSON

<u>Chapter One</u>

Tom Petty's *Free Fallin'* hums through my old clock radio, waking me up from a deep sleep. I've heard that the sight of waking up is fairly different than feeling, hearing, smelling, and tasting the morning. . . . I can do those four, but seeing is something I cannot do.

I know the savory feeling of morning; it is the warm sun against your skin coming through the prismatic glass of the windows and the silk of the bed sheets wrapping around your legs. The sound of a bird's muffled chirping outside of your window or the first footsteps of someone else in the house are the sounds of dawn. Bacon and eggs can easily be the first scent that you smell when your eyes flutter open. The taste at daybreak is the bitterness of morning breath and warm coffee; the cool mint of toothpaste usually following it (at least, I hope so).

Saturday mornings are the kind of mornings that I remember dearly. Cartoons and saccharine cereal for breakfast and staying in my pajamas well past noon—a vivid childhood memory. I am able to remember that *today* is Saturday, but it won't be the same. It will be the same emptiness I see every single day. I'm thankful, though, that I wake up to see a new day. Some people don't get a chance to wake up, and there isn't a difference between the darkness that they see and the darkness I see.

They are both eternal but they're dead and I'm not. Saturdays are another fat 'X' marked on my calendar.

Only slivers of my mind remember what certain things look like from before I went blind: faces and items from our house and our neighborhood route, but my grandparents have rearranged things over the years. I like to go over the shelves with my hands and feel the picture frames that are propped up. There is one particular photo that sticks out of one picture frame—it's small and it's stuck in the crease of the frame. It's wrinkly and thin. I've asked Grandma who or what is in the photo but she tells me it's an old picture of me when I was a kid. I can also recall colors but it is hard to remember the tints and shades that each color holds. I presume my memory will get a lot worse in the future. If someone were to say a color, I'd most likely be able to recollect it by associating it with an object—like the color green reminds me of grass and leaves. My imagination makes up the rest. I have everything in the house memorized so I don't run into things. Grandma tries not to move anything that might throw my natural balance off.

I don't remember the accident itself or how it occurred, but I do remember very small things before it and sometimes have vague flashbacks. The strongest memory I have out of all of them is of my mother. I know that she died, and it was before I went blind, so I remember her appearance to an extent. Her electric blue eyes were strikingly soft, yet fierce along with her very sharp features; she pops up in my dreams once in awhile, appearing the same, sometimes along with the other girl. I also know that I have a father, but I don't remember him.

At all.

I don't know if he is alive or dead; I don't know what he did after mom died. I don't know where he went after I went blind, either. Grandma and Grandpa have barely talked about him with me, despite all of the questions I have asked. After Grandma's usual freak-out fits whenever I question her about my mother and father's relationship, I quit asking. The only subject they are willing to discuss is my mother, and I don't have a problem with that. Sometimes I think they're hiding things from me, though.

The last time I actually *saw* my grandparents with my own eyes was before I was in the hospital and they looked very young for their age. They sound and feel a lot older now, but their smells have not changed much.

Grandma went back to smoking again a while after she took me in so her voice is much hoarser and shriller. I always feel bad because I feel like I am the cause of her nicotine addiction. Grandpa's slippers dragging across the wooden floor and the way he clears his throat of mucus after every meal is tattooed into my eardrums. Grandma has quick and steady footsteps; that's how I tell both of them apart when I'm in a different room. She also doesn't clear her throat—she coughs it completely up. Thus, a smoker's cough is interpreted much more alarmingly by a blind person. They both smell like old people, of course, yet their scents are very much different from each other.

At first, I expected Grandma to smell like smoke most of the time; in reality she just smells like a mustier version of *Sunflower* by Elizabeth Arden. Every time I hug her, the wrinkles in her blouse release the scent in bursts, making my sensitive nose tingle. Grandpa smells of Old Spice aftershave and coffee, and I can smell both mixing together at the same time whenever I go to kiss him on his shaven, powdery cheek. He is constantly drinking coffee throughout the day, decaf or not, and the smell of it lingers on him like a perpetual cloud.

It is typical for blind people to feel an individual's face to map out what they look like; but it is also typical for blind people not to care what others look like in the

first place. When someone is able to notice that I cannot see them and their movements—even though I can surely feel them—they are very cautious. I can tell by the change in the way they breathe, if they are close enough, and whether or not I can feel them move away from me or closer. I think that is what irks me the most. *I'm* the one who can't see in this situation, so why are you the one to be cautious of me?

There was one night in particular after dinner as Grandma, Grandpa, and I all sat in front of a television that I could only hear, and asked them if I could feel their faces. Silence settled after I heard Grandpa stand to turn the television off and I could feel the awkwardness float through the air. I wanted to feel what they looked like presently, because I was curious to find out if they had changed over the years. A wrinkly, yet soft hand grabbed my own shaky hand—I immediately sensed that it was Grandma's hand because of her rings—and gently laid my fingers onto her face. I could feel her warm breath on my palm and I pictured her young face from ten years ago, but more wrinkled and rough. I remembered that she had reddish—brown hair, but I assumed that there were shiny gray streaks in it by now. I moved my fingers over her lips, feeling the natural pucker and smoker's lines.

She had round eyes and full eyebrows. The brow

bone was sharp yet delicate; same as her nose. I smiled and moved my hand back down to her lips again, feeling her wide smile. Her cheeks were soft, but at this point they were also wet.

I brought my hand down and hugged her as she hugged me back, feeling the vibration and shaking of her thin spine as she cried. This was the first time I'd witnessed Grandma cry. I wasn't sure how to react, so I just sat there and comforted her, feeling the guilt flood my throbbing, pained heart. I felt so bad, I swear I could feel my heart's tendons tearing, its fibers floating down my chest and sticking its sadness to the walls of my stomach.

Grandma didn't deserve this. She didn't deserve me—a blind, naive girl who could barely feel for the buttons on the voicemail machine. I ruined her and I could feel it. Her pajama shirt was soft and warm from her body heat as I rubbed her stiff back.

I heard Grandpa stand up again and walk over, his slippers slowly sliding against the floor, eventually wrapping his arms around us. I felt his face with my shaking palms briefly while he was hugging us, as I did not want to let go of Grandma. He had a chiseled facial structure but I felt his aging, plump cheeks and I realized that he had a coarse line of hair above his upper lip. I don't recall him having a mustache before, but I giggled a bit at the feel of it and I could feel his lips turn up into sly smile. I felt Grandma slip from the hug just enough to put her fingers above mine to his lips as well.

She sniffled a bit but then began to giggle, her voice still thick with sadness as she inquired, "His mustache does feel a little funny, doesn't it? You should see it." We all knew I couldn't.

For the rest of that night, we talked about Grandpa's mustache and the infamous story about how everyone thought he looked like John Waters in the eighties. I didn't know what John Waters looked like, but ironically, I could understand his famous features through Grandpa.

Tom Petty still rings soothingly against my ears through the radio as I stretch my legs and flip the covers over to get up. I feel around for the umbrella that serves as my walking stick, and make sure there isn't anything on the floor before standing up. I don't like using a normal walking stick because it calls too much attention to me; the umbrella is more inconspicuous. The floors throughout the house are always clean for safety measures, because less than a year after I became blind and was still getting used to my surroundings, there was a mouse I didn't know about creeping throughout my room. Apparently he was there for over a month making himself at home—until one day I stepped on him coming home from the farmer's market with Grandma. I remember screeching and feeling his small body squish slightly underneath my heel.

As I backed out of my room sobbing, I heard Grandpa pick up the mouse with his bare hands as he hugged me and told me that it wasn't my fault. I cried and cried and cried, thinking that it obviously was because I was the one who stepped on it, but one thing that Grandpa told me about the mouse that I'll never forget: "Watching your step is important; but watching what's in your step is even more impactful." I noticed a peculiar smell at the time, so it *did* make some sense. I've always felt bad for that mouse, but at least I learned a good life lesson from it. After that, Grandpa let me be a kid and give it a small funeral. He buried it next to Grandma's rose bush and I invited Ryker and Christine to it.

It is now a habit of mine to check the floors before I walk on them. I'm not the only crazy person in my house. I sure am the only blind one, though.

As I walk towards the large door to the bathroom, I sense Grandpa in the hallway.

"Hi, Pops," I say, leaning against the umbrella.

I hear him clear his throat before answering. "Morning, my Orca," he replies, using my childhood nickname. I smile lightly and reach out for his arm, hugging it. His plush robe feels nice against my cold arms.

He kisses my head and walks off lightly, humming.

I feel his steps under mine against the wooden floors as he turns right, towards the living room and kitchen where Grandma is cooking. I hear the pans clink together above Grandpa's light singing as I trudge to the bathroom and shut the door quietly behind me. I lean the umbrella against the wall and go to the sink, sliding my hands against the taps as I grab the bar of soap. The hot tap has a 3-D letter 'H' on it and the cold tap has a 'C'. I turn both of them on to create warm water and cup my hands under the tap, the warmth spreading throughout my fingers and up my arms. I splash my face and lather the soap into a creamy foam before rubbing it gently on my face, feeling all of my features.

My eyes are wide and almond-shaped, my cheeks are soft except for a few acne bumps here and there. My lips are full but I still have a very small scar from the accident indenting the middle of my bottom lip, causing it to feel more plush—it feels like a soft indent in a peach. I know that my eyes are green, but I am not sure what hue of green exactly. My brow bone is on the softer side, and my eyebrows are thin and natural. Grandma plucks them for me every now and then whenever she notices them growing thicker. I definitely can feel that my features have aged over the last ten years since I saw myself before the accident.

I think that being so young when everything happened has tainted my memories a bit; and that it is very different than waking up and seeing nothing again. In my dreams, I am able to see everything normally. People, colors, nature . . . I am able to see everything I could ever imagine once my eyes flutter shut for the night.

It is one hell of an experience.

One of the most vibrant dreams that I have had (ever since they started) took place underwater, the waves flowing like air around me.

I discover that I can breathe normally, my eyes fluttering open and around the crystal blue landscape I float in as I regain consciousness. I'm not scared; everything is calm. There are no tides and the soft, grainy sand isn't swirling everywhere. Everything floats gently against the bright sunlight beaming through the waves. The crystal sun casts my shadow on a large, swaying bundle of seaweed tangled up against a rock and I realize that I have a dress on.

The dress sways in sync with the plants as the waves twirl it into a silky ribbon that swirls all around me. Its cascade of softness grazes my legs and I feel comfortable; everything is happening in slow-motion, like time is in a trance within the clear, warm water. I see bubbles float out of the corner of my eye and turn, taking a deep breath. Two females float, nearly nude, and one looks older than the other. They are looking at each other and it seems like they are holding their breath, unlike me. I swim quickly towards them and grab the younger girl's arm, her face coming very close to mine.

She looks like me.

I try to push her up to the surface but once she reaches the top, the side of her head bumps against the blue, shimmering surface as if there was a glass barrier. I look over at the older woman and she just gazes at me with a sympathy I can't understand. She looks like the younger girl, who looks like me, so technically I look like her. She is drowning and she is giving me the saddest look; and it isn't because she is sad. She isn't sad she's drowning, at the fact that she can't breathe.

She's sad that I am living.

I try to grab her and push her up to the surface too, but she just holds onto my arms as we float. I feel the back of my legs float upwards, my hands balancing on her arms as she holds me up, her blue eyes glistening in the sun, the water making them look like blinking tanzanite jewels. The sun is so bright that the crystal blue water isn't noticeably blue anymore and it looks like we are floating in white-hot liquid glass.

She holds me until I can't tell if the liquid near my eyes is water or tears. I feel pain—the pain that she is radiating onto me—as my sobs are muffled under the water and she pulls me slowly closer, the water like syrup. I look over the older woman's shoulder, my eyes cloudy, and notice that the younger girl is gone. I look around frantically until I see the older woman laying in the sand, the waves coming stronger now, and swirling the sand around her until her body is covered. Her face is white and I can't see her tanzanite eyes any longer.

I rinse the soap off of my face and feel for a towel on the metal towel rack beside me, grabbing the softest one and patting my face dry. I reach into the cabinet and grab my toothbrush with three thick dots on the base of it—which help indicate which toothbrush is mine—and the toothpaste, and begin to brush my teeth, the mint shocking my taste buds and burning my nose slightly. Once I finish, I grab the comb that Grandma always places beside the hand soap and start combing through my tangled locks. My hair is short—about shoulder length—and curly. It feels much shorter though because its inevitable frizziness and curls mask the length.

The girl in my dream has the same kind of hair that I do, except I noticed that it is a bit longer than mine; her hair goes to her collarbones. She is young, though—she looks around twelve. I assume that was what I looked like at that age, over five years ago.

I know the type of blond hair that we share: strawberry. From what I remember of when *I* was younger, it looked white and wasn't as voluminous. The girl in my dreams' hair is a lot lighter than mine. Her hair reminds me of the white seed heads on dandelions that you can blow and make a wish on. Grandma tells me that my hair is a very light peachy cream color and that each strand reminds her of peony petals.

I grab the closed umbrella when I am done, slide it against the floor outside of the bathroom to check to make sure I'm not going to bump into Grandma or Grandpa, and go back to my room to dress. The radio now fuzzes in and out as a talk-show host rambles, so I just shut it off completely as I go to my dresser and once again drop the umbrella lazily to the floor.

The way I pick my clothes out of the dresser is by the individual drawer. My dresser has four drawers, in order from top to bottom: shirts and flannels, pants, pajamas, and undergarments. My shirts are mainly band T-shirts or plain T-shirts, along with simple flannels, that are easy to match to my pants because all of my selected pants are blue jeans or sweatpants. I trust Ryker with picking out my band shirts for me whenever we are able to go shopping because we both have the same (awesome) taste in music. I'm glad he doesn't mind shopping with me.

Fabric is also a very big part of how I pick and choose my clothing, typically because I can't see it but also because I want to make sure I like the fabric and that it won't be itchy.

I reach for the top drawer, my T-shirts, and grab the first one. I can feel the thin vinyl design on the front, indicating that it is a band shirt. I slide on the t-shirt effortlessly, making sure to feel for the tag so I don't put it on backwards. I go to the second drawer and feel for my favorite distressed jeans; they are the most comfortable pair I own. I can feel the holes on the knee and thighs of the fabric. Ryker told me when I bought them that they have light bleach-like splatters on them.

I feel for the tag once again inside of the waistline and put them on and feel the cuffs of the jeans, making sure that they aren't uneven. I grab a pair of clean socks and slip them on. I feel on top of my dresser, which is where I put my deodorant and various body sprays. I apply deodorant, its floral scent wafting to my nose quickly. I grab one of the body spray bottles and smell it carefully and spray some lightly on my neck and wrists, its sweet and earthy scent filling the room.

Once I finish with everything, I grab my umbrella and a thin jean jacket. I walk out of my bedroom making sure there isn't anything on the ground and close the door behind me. I feel tired still; even though I went to bed early the night before in order to dream. I always look forward to dreaming; mainly because it is my own personal sanctuary that nobody knows about. Grandma and Grandpa don't *truly* know about the bizarre dreams I experience. We've been to counseling before and I've tried explaining it to them but they don't understand. It's mainly Grandma who refuses to listen. I have tried telling Ryker about it before too, when the dreams first started occurring when I was ten, three years after the accident, but we both shrugged it off and convinced ourselves it wasn't real, even though I knew it really was. I'm not sure if Ryker ever thinks about it, let alone remembers what I told him. I think it'd be best if I keep it to myself.

I make my way towards the kitchen, the warm, roasted smell of coffee and hazelnut whirling in the air along with the fresh, bubbly aroma of dish soap as I hear Grandma washing last night's dishes; plates and silverware clinking together. I hear Grandpa sit in his favorite chair, the scuffle of his slippers and the creaking of the seat echoes against the wooden floor. I walk over to Grandma and put my hand on her shoulder. She puts her warm, soapy hand over mine.

"Good morning, Grandma," I say, kissing her warm cheek. I smell cigarette smoke on her breath. "Do you know what time it is?"

"Good morning, Orchid Jane. It is almost noon, dear," she says as she continues to wash dishes. I cringe at my middle name. I walk over to the countertop on the left and feel for the coffee pot. I take a clean mug from the dry dish rack and carefully pour coffee. Just the smell of it wakes me up. I decide to grab an extra cup for Grandpa.

"Aren't you going over to Ryker's today? It's Saturday, right?" Grandpa asks as I walk over to his chair cautiously and hand him his cup. I feel for his hand, making sure he has a steady grip on the mug so I won't spill hot coffee all over him.

"Yeah, Pops. Guitar practice is every Saturday." I reply. I hear him clear his throat in approval. Ryker plays guitar *extremely* well and a couple months ago we made a bet that if I didn't wear any band shirts for one week, he wouldn't have to teach me guitar over the summer. I lost, of course. I remember getting a little upset over it because I thought he was using my impairment against me; but overall, I lost on purpose. I can tell right away if a shirt of mine has a band logo on it just by the feeling of the fabric itself, regardless of if I can or cannot tell *which* band it is.

"I always forget what day it is, Orca! I have you to remind me." the smile in his voice beams through my eardrums and I smile a bit, too. Grandpa has an innocence to him that will never perish. Grandma is the exact opposite; she knows everything about anything in the world. She hides things; and when things don't go her way, she isn't happy. Grandpa chooses to ignore certain things that don't improve his life; I think that is what brings us together the most.

"Gerald, leave that poor girl alone . . . you know damn well it is Saturday, plum. . . ," Grandma chastises gently, and Grandpa chuckles quietly.

I walk over to the kitchen table and sit down in the same wooden seat I always sit in. We all have our own chairs but Grandpa usually sits in his recliner and Grandma sometimes sits with me if she feels like it.

I take a sip of my coffee, its bitterness infecting my taste buds and making my nose scrunch up. I grab the cream from the middle of the table and cautiously pour some, feeling the spout on the pitcher. I feel for the rough sugar cubes and plop a couple in, a little bit of coffee splattering onto my palm. I stir it a bit more and take a sip, then I hear the phone ring.

The phone hangs on the wall beside the refrigerator and I jump at the loud, shrill ring it emits.

Even after ten years, that phone still scares me.

I get up and go over to the fridge a few feet before

me and grab the phone cord, its rubber spirals vibrating with every ring.

"Hello?"

Orc," a male voice rumbles through the phone. "Are you ready to play some jams?" he asks. I can hear him smile. I can also hear Nirvana blasting in the background. "Yes, Ryker," I bite back sarcastically, "Certainly not here to make jelly," I lean against the wall beside me. "Now I'm just waiting on your ass." I chuckle when Grandma huffs in disapproval.

"Alright, alright, I'll be there in fifteen." I hear him crunching on something. The boy eats like a pig.

"You live two blocks away from me,"

"And?"

I roll my eyes. "See you soon, *Teenage Dirtbag*."

We like to refer to each other with vintage songs and movies. It's the holy grail of our friendship.

"Um, I hate to burst your bubble, but technically you won't, *Princess Bride*," I hear him laugh through the receiver, his voice rasping with mirth. His voice is either rough like peanut brittle or smooth as caramel. Either way, it always makes me melt.

I also hear Ryker's mom, Christine, snap at him to

24

get off the phone because she needs to use it.

"I was just joking, Orch—" his voice distances from the phone for a second, arguing with Christine. I hear her tell him to turn the blaring music down.

His voice finally comes back to the receiver, the music a lot fainter, and he is annoyed.

"Alright, Ma, I'm going!" I hear Ryker grab his car keys as he sighs. The fact that he is picking me up when he lives literally less than ten minutes walking distance is beyond me.

"See you in a few, Orc." the line rings dead. I sigh as a small smile forms upon my lips, feeling a presence behind me. I move over a bit and smell coffee.

"That boy Ryker sure has one helluva stereo, I could hear his music all the way over here through the phone." Grandpa states.

I nod my head in agreement even though he was right behind me when I was talking to Ryker.

The funny thing about our friendship—on my part, frankly—is that it is the only friendship I've truly had. Kids around our neighborhood when we were younger never wanted anything to do with me, and when I became blind, that really cut the cake. Thickly.

I take the last chug of my coffee and rinse my mug off in the sink, hoping that it won't take him forever. Even though I just heard him munching on some sort of junk food, he will most likely stop by Daisy Doughnuts on his way here. I have always wondered if he ended up weighing three hundred pounds after I became blind (even though it doesn't really matter since I'd love him either way).

I sit back down at the kitchen table, listening to the television while also keeping an ear out for Ryker's car. Grandpa is watching a rerun of Forensic Files and it doesn't interest me too much, so I lay my head down until I hear a rough turn into the gravel driveway.

I walk outside, the thin umbrella in my hand and Ryker's muffler growling as the sound of it leads me to his car. I hear him get out and open the door for me, faint music and air conditioning greeting me as I sit down. The smell of Royal Pine car freshener and fried, sugary dough invade my senses.

"I better get one of these doughnuts, *Poppin' Fresh*," I say as he gets in the car. He chuckles and lays the box on my lap.

"Don't get your grubby fingers all over them, I told Mom I'd leave her a few." I feel the car move as I smile and pick the first one I touch, its warm and crumbly dough starting to fall apart in my hand. Taking a colossal bite, the sugar coats my tongue as its jelly bursts forth into my mouth. It's grape in all its glory.

"Christine wouldn't mind me taking the jelly one, would she?" I ask, my mouth full of gooey doughnut.

"Of course not, though it is a little late now," he says. "If I were the one to take it, though, she probably would care. Grape is her favorite."

"I'll make sure to tell her you were the one who ate it, then."

"Yeah, do that while you have jelly on your cheek." he deadpans. His finger rubs up against my cheek suddenly and wipes away the apparent chunk of jelly. I hear him lick his finger and turn up the radio.

****

We are sitting in Ryker's basement practicing the G-chord when his mom comes down with the phone for him. He says he'll be right back as his footsteps thump up the stairs, his voice echoing against the door. I figure it is one of his buddies.

Ryker has always had a lot more friends than I have, and he met even more once we entered high school. Some not-so particularly good ones in my opinion, but they are still his friends.

I figured it was just because of the fact I was blind, but I realized after a while that I don't associate myself with people as much as I should in the first place. I did have one acquaintance besides Ryker, though. My junior year last year, I met a girl named Penelope in my horticulture class. She was a foreign exchange student from England and we were partners for three months until she was shipped back to her hometown in Bath. I guess the family she was staying with here wasn't good enough for her parents, and they forced her out immediately once they found out the host mom worked as a business woman during the day, but a stripper at night. I'm still not sure who Penelope stayed with, but I think that part was supposed to stay a secret. At least for a while, I had someone to dig up the worms I always avoided in class.

It is a bit more difficult to communicate when everyone at school ignores me, but at least I had Ryker as a lunch buddy who gave me his extra ranch packets while we were still in school. I hope it will be the same way next year.

I lean back into the couch and rub my sore fingers as

I feel it shift with weight beside me. I smell lavender perfume.

"Ryker isn't hounding you too much on the G chord, is he?" Christine giggles.

"Not really, besides the bleeding fingers and burning wrists from holding his guitar for so long, it's going great."

She laughs and it instantly reminds me of when Ryker and I were younger. I can't recall much of anything before the accident but I know that she has always had the same voice and laugh; it seems like nothing has changed about Christine over the last ten years. After my mom died, she began to treat me like her own. She has always been the anchor of our family. She also works as an accountant and I'm actually surprised she's home right now. Anywho, she never takes shit from anyone. "Pretty soon you'll be a pro at it. Ryker is thinking about entering in the town's local guitar competition for young guitarists." she says. I smile, not surprised, even though I have never noticed our small town here in Florida hosting a guitarist competition. Nonetheless, it seems interesting to me.

"He never mentioned that to me but I think he should enter. He would totally kill it!" I exclaim. "When is it?"

"In a couple of weeks," Christine says. "Maybe when you get a little better at it, you can join him." she suggests.

I shrug. "I don't want to take his spotlight. I don't think I'll become that good in time for the show, anyways,"

"Honey, you really should start putting yourself out there,"

I begin to feel a little defensive as she says this. "I do, I just think this whole guitar thing is more fit for Ryker. Maybe once I find something I really like to do, I will."

I feel her hand on my knee comfortingly as she stands up and sighs.

"I know. You're an amazing girl, I just don't want you to always think that Ryker is able to do anything and everything that *you* think *you* can't or aren't able to do. Hell, he can barely put his dirty clothes in the right hamper when I ask him to," she says and I laugh. "You can do anything you want to do, as long as you put your mind to it, Orchid."

I smile, even though I secretly think that that saying is really cheesy. I hold my arms out for a hug, her warm

THE SOUND OF RAIN

embrace flooding my veins as she hugs back.

"I'm gone for five minutes and my basement turns into an intervention room?" I hear Ryker ask, his voice echoing against the walls.

"Technically it's my basement, sweets," Christine retorts, her footsteps echoing up the staircase. Ryker sits back down next to me.

"Who was that on the phone?" I ask as I feel him rub up against my leg as he situates himself back on the couch.

"It was Carson," he says, picking up the guitar at my feet and strumming carelessly. "He invited me to a party."

"Oh, cool," I reply casually. Carson is one of the more popular guys at school. I've met him before at a school assembly through Ryker and he seems okay. I have no clue what he looks like but I figure he is probably cute, despite how cocky he is.

Ryker isn't in Carson's little clique, but he does attend a lot of their activities. And by activities, I mean parties that include guitar riff-offs in the back of an abandoned gas station that is a few blocks away from town. They have other parties at Carson's house too, and apparently that is where this one is being held. They also drink sometimes.

I'm not surprised that he was invited to yet another party; but I *am* surprised when he asks me to come with him.

"I don't know. . . ," I hesitate. My heart beats faster with nervousness. I have never been to an actual high school party before. Technically, this is a *summer* high school party, but still. The only parties I've attended were family-related or for birthdays.

"Come on, it'll be fun. I'll help you find something cute to wear," he says, his voice growing high and pitchy on the last part.

I laugh. "I don't think he'd want me there, anyways."

"Why would you think that?" he asks.

I don't really answer him; I just tell him that I will think about it instead. A part of me wants to but another part of me is really pulling back. I'm nervous I'll screw something up and being around so many strange people just doesn't sound inviting to me. I think it is because I am not used to being invited to many events and my thoughts are just swarming around out of spite.

I pick at my guitar to change the subject and Ryker

places my fingers in certain spots.

"Can I feel your guitar?" I ask. I've never played *his* guitar.

"Sure."

I take the one I currently have off and he places the guitar around my neck, the pressure of the strap a little heavier than the other one.

"Do you know what her name is?"

"It's a her?"

"You bet. Her name is Lucy Diamond and she's a beauty."

"I do bet. Where did you come up with the name?"

"The Beatles' *Lucy in the Sky with Diamonds*."

"Clever."

"One of my favorites. Alright, place your fingers here . . . and here . . . ," he helps me situate my hands. "Okay good, now strum."

As we continue to play, I think about what Christine said. Maybe she is right—I feel like I never really go out anywhere besides being with Ryker and the occasional stroll by myself.

I want change; and boy, will it come.

****

Later that night I lay in bed, trying to fall asleep. I hear the television out in the living room, my grandparents watching some sort of action movie with a lot of cursing
and explosions. I try to block it out, but it's no use. I turn my radio on and turn the volume down low enough so only I can hear it. Coldplay's *Yellow* floats in the air like a rich, majestic cloud . . . which lulls me to into a vivid, deep sleep.

There are two mirrors leaning against a willow tree. The mirrors are covered in vines and a girl is standing in front of the one on my right. From what I am able to see from this particular perspective, I'm behind a rose bush, completely mesmerized. Everything is vibrant in color, like every branch and leaf is coated in candy, and I feel as if I am to bite into a leaf it would taste like a green apple lollipop. I also undeniably feel that I am intruding on a fairy's land, swarming deep within its beauty as the weeping willow tree hangs gracefully above her and the mirrors, giving the scenery a peaceful feeling.

A few long moments later, she is still standing there. The only thing that moves on her petite body is her lace dress and thin, blond hair, which follows the gusts of wind as if she is floating in water. It is very spectral; a chill runs up my spine.

I finally get the courage to rise to my feet, the rose bush rustling underneath me, wafting a dewy rose petal scent throughout the chilly air. It is a strong scent and it makes my nose itch. The girl is still looking in the mirror, and I can see only part of her face. It is pale and it's slightly heart shaped. Her emotionless expression as she stares in the mirror makes me wonder what she is thinking about. I can't tell if she is staring at herself or the objects behind her; but I mostly hope that she can't see me.

I carefully step away from the rose bushes, a couple loose thorns and branches sticking my feet as I crunch past. I ignore the pain shooting through the soles of my feet; I am too intrigued to feel pain at the moment. As I inch closer to the girl and the mirror, I see that her eyes are green and they continuously keep shaking; like she is in a demented trance. Her mouth is partially open, showing a missing front tooth. I walk closer to her, holding my breath, and that is when she stops. It feels like less than a split second later when all she does is close her eyes and hang her head. I watch her, standing next to her now, only the rustle of the trees and branches making light swooshing sounds against the wind. A few pink and deep red rose petals are swept up from the ground by another strong gust of wind, causing them to float around us. It reminds me of bloody rain.

I take a small breath but hold it once her head shoots up and she looks right at me. She looks innocent, standing there with her eyes looking right into mine; the green around her pupil burning to a dark juniper. I feel the guilt squirm within my chest. She looks trapped; like she doesn't know what to do with herself or how to get out of here. She doesn't seem terrified but I know that she doesn't like being here at all. My eyebrows furrow with curiosity as she lifts her hand gently and cups the back of my neck—its coolness makes me shiver. Anxious goosebumps form on my arms as she turns my head slightly towards the mirror she is standing in front of. I can't see her figure anymore. It is just me.

I realize that we form together as one and I stare at myself in the mirror in horror. I am wearing the same thing as she is wearing; I can see the puffy outline of her dress flowing against mine. She still has her hand on the back of my neck, and I can feel her grip tighten against the veins lining my neck. I lift my own hand up hesitantly up to hers, wanting to tell her to stop, but she thrusts my face up to the mirror. I gasp.

My face is so close to colliding with the mirror, but just the tip of my nose touches the cool glass. It reflects my features but not myself. I feel different as I look at myself more closely this time, noticing that my eyes are fading to a rosy color, and eventually into a garnet red. I try to pull back, but she thrusts my head forward again, this time into the glass, causing it to shatter. I squeeze my eyes shut, feeling the glass scrape my face. I feel her force lighten, as if she disappeared.

I feel a warm liquid running down my forehead and

THE SOUND OF RAIN

assume it is blood from the glass cutting me. I also feel a few burning streaks on my cheeks and chin, and it stings a little bit as I wipe my forehead and look at all of the glass on the ground. I don't want to cut my feet.

I pick up small shards of glass silently, looking around for the girl. I find a large shard of glass as big as my face and look into it. The gash is still there; and my eyes are still red within the irises. I close my eyes with the glass against my burning forehead and feel a tender, cold hand grasp my face again as I wake up.

Everything is black when my eyes open. I can still see faint silhouettes of the trees and their lime-green leaves waving gently against the unlit normality I always see, like they are saying goodbye. I quietly say goodbye, too, even though that wouldn't be the last time that I see the girl nor that crisp, mysterious forest and the broken glass that litters it.

Throughout the rest of the week, Ryker and I hang out back and forth at each other's houses as Florida's heat warns us to stay inside. We practice guitar, eat food, and . . . well, that's basically it.

Grandma goes outside in the summer to garden and I feel bad for her once this heat wave moves in. Her flowers are starting to dry out and we won't hear the end of it until Grandpa buys her more to plant from our local greenhouse, so I go with him once it is cool enough to leave the house (or more like when the temperature is below the nineties).

"Orchid, do you know what Grandma's favorite flower is?" he asks me as we walk slowly down the aisles of flowers and plants, their petals and leaves brushing against both sides of my arms, making them itch. I hold onto my closed umbrella, making sure that there isn't anything littering the ground that I could trip on. I hear Grandpa slide a pot over on the ground to get it out of my way while the plants create a thick and earthy atmosphere around us. It makes me feel warmer than I already am. "No, I thought she liked all flowers." I reply. It is rare for Grandpa to ever say my full name.

Grandma has always gardened; and when I was able to see, I remember the fairy garden she had and the enormous amount of flowers of all sorts that scattered the ground in colorful bundles. The garden fades out into a large, empty field. She has so many flowers, I figured she didn't have a favorite.

"Her favorite flowers are orchids," he says and I smile, letting out a relieved sigh. It wasn't about something too serious, after all. "Back when we got married, a long, long time ago, the first flower I ever gave your grandmother was, in fact, an orchid." I can hear the smile in his voice.

"Your mother named you after an orchid because that was the first flower *your* father gave your mother, too . . . and of course, your grandmother wanted a say in the name. . . ," he continues.

Shocked, I stand there and listen. This is the first time that I'm hearing of this information; but it makes me kind of . . . well, happy. I'm starting to get a little nervous again, though.

I'm kind of scared at first once he begins telling me the origin of my name because I keep thinking that Grandma will find out. I am never to be told anything too serious. I know Grandpa could keep secrets but it is probably difficult keeping them from Grandma and I can understand that easily.

If she does find out. . . .

But he also doesn't sound like he cares too much whether or not Grandma finds out at all. "Here, hold this," he says, suddenly cutting himself off. A large hunk of cement lands in my palms; and I realize that it is a planting pot after I feel the thin layer of dirt inside it.

I hear his voice echo against the walls along with his footsteps as he makes his way further down the aisle.

"Start picking out some flowers if you wish, Orca," he says, putting a few anonymous plants he picked on his own in.

I feel the flowers as I walk slowly down the aisle myself. I try to feel for the softest ones; or the ones that I think smell the best. I find one particular plant that make my fingers sting.

I gasp with pain, almost dropping the plant and the pot. I wipe my hand on my jeans and lean over to smell the plant carefully; and it's light, sweet, and earthy scent floated around me, caressing my nostrils as I ask Grandpa to come over to me.

I'm careful not to feel the stem and I feel the petals, their velvety curves and curls wrapping around my finger. "Ah, a rose," Grandpa claims quietly. I pick a few of them off of the small bush, still avoiding the toxic stems, and feel for Grandpa's thin, wrinkly hand. I lay them down on his palm gently until I hear him yelp. I pull back, startled. "Those roses really do getcha, Orca," he says, wheezing. I panic for a second, thinking he is having a hard time breathing, but I figure out that he is laughing and I giggle a bit, too.

"Roses are like people, you know," he continues as I stay silent, listening with intent. "They find a way to hide their own personal truth with their beauty and softness, but once you handle them in the wrong way, their thorns always find a way to stick out."

****

Once Grandpa and I get home, we give Grandma her flowers and I help her replant them for the rest of the afternoon. When we are finished, she helps me scrub the dirt out from underneath my nails and place some of the roses in a vase on the kitchen table.

"What time is it?" I ask Grandma as I feel her scrub my knuckles gently.

"The sun is setting," she replies, clearing her throat. "The orange in the sky is mixing with the blue and it is fading." I remember orange from the sun itself and blue from the water in my dream. I begin imagining the big orange sun setting in the ocean I was trapped in. Sunsets mean the end of the day.

"Just like a big 'ol sweet apple pie, Denise." Grandpa chimes in, talking to Grandma, as his slippers slide behind me. Grandma laughs softly and finishes scrubbing my hands. I could still feel small chunks of dirt deep under my nail but it didn't bother me. When I go grab a towel to pat them dry, I hear a knock at the door. "Oh, Dean! What a surprise. Can I help you?" I hear
Grandma ask. She sounds a bit worried. I stay silent,

still drying my hands, my back towards them. *Does she mean Officer Dean? From the farmer's market?* "Ah, Mrs. Dahl, good evening," a husky voice replies. He sounds sort of old but not as old as Grandma and Grandpa. I think he is in his mid-forties; or at least that's what Grandma told me. Besides Grandpa always being her true love, I think she has a minor crush on Officer Dean. I am assuming he is eye candy for her and I wish I can say the same. "Do you mind if I step inside for a moment?"

"Come on in," I hear the door creak shut as Grandma and the police officer make their way towards the living room. "Would you like something to eat or drink?" "No, thank you, Maisy made dinner already." he chuckles.

"Oh, isn't she ready to pop yet? What is she having? Twins?"

"She's great, she isn't due until August. . . ," As their conversation continues, I stand still in the kitchen with curiosity. I wonder if anyone got murdered in town—no, that couldn't be . . . Grandma would have heard it on the local news and blabbed by now. If it was big enough, maybe it'd even be on the national news.

Wow, the only time Oath would be famous is through a tragedy.

What if there is a child missing? Or maybe a dog? What if it is something to do with Ryker?

Oh, God. I really hope it has nothing to do with Ryker.

Worry and anxiety consumes me as they sit in there, chitchatting away about his pregnant wife and how good the tomatoes are this year at the market. I turn, grab my umbrella near the edge of the bottom cupboard, and make my way over to the kitchen table. I think they notice because there is an awkward pause until Officer Dean says hi to me.

"Hello," I reply. I can tell he is a bit closer than before just from his vocal range but he is still in the living room.

"Anyways, I came here to talk to you and Gerald about something," he ignores my greeting and I hear him get something out of his pocket. I turn back around and roll my eyes with annoyance. From it's crinkling, it sort of sounded like a piece of paper or a picture. I still keep my ears open as they talk. They bring their voices down to a whisper.

"He's back in town," Grandma whispers, sounding shocked. *Who?*

"Here is a photo from a few months back. Caught in

Georgia for domestic violence on multiple accounts towards some druggie friends of his living with him . . . he made his way through Florida at some point over the last week or so."

"It's been years," Grandma replies, gasping.

"I figured I'd come over here personally and warn you folks."

The whispers continue as the shock and worry throughout the room grows stronger. I'm extremely curious. I want to know who they are talking about. Hell, I want to see the picture, too!

The couch cushions squeak as they stand up, Officer Dean beginning leave. I hear Grandma and Grandpa say goodbye as Officer Dean walks past me to go through the back door, out of the kitchen. I feel a large hand on my shoulder as he passes.

"Take care, Orchid," Officer Dean says. I smile.

"Thanks, you too. Tell Maisy I say hi."

"Will do, sweetheart."

The door creaks shut and I relax a bit. Grandma and Grandpa go back to watching television like normal and I sit there in the old wooden chair until my butt starts to hurt, trying to figure out who they were talking about. I don't dare ask right then and there, though. Maybe I could try asking in the morning when Grandma is half asleep.

I grab my umbrella and make my way towards my bedroom and get ready for bed. I'm suddenly extremely tired and although I'm still a little worked up from Officer Dean's visit, it really wore me out at the same time. After I brush my teeth and comb my hair, I slide into the cool covers of my bed and switch on my radio quietly. I barely have enough time to figure out what song is playing before I fall into a deep sleep. This night is the last night that I will be calm enough to immediately fall asleep.

It is also the first night in a number of years that I never even have a dream.

HANA FERGUSON

HANA FERGUSON

Chapter Two

Oathpark is the type of town where everyone knows everybody. We all greet each other the same, we all know each other's problems, and most of all, the gossip travels like a wildfire.

No one has ever talked about the accident that I was in as a child; at least as far as I've been a teenager. Once in a blue moon I'll hear faint mutters at the market.

I've tried so hard to remember before the accident, but I can't. This town makes it difficult to remember anything. A bitterness has grown on me like moss and it clogs my ears whenever I go anywhere. Talking to the people in this town is barely feasible because I feel like I'm talking to robots everywhere. A part of me is glad that I can't see the people around me because they all probably have malfunctioned faces that drip with green lies and gold tears. People don't care much about other people here. People care about everything but people.

A bubble of mint and flawlessness clouds the town and everyone acts like they have perfect lives around us, but they don't. Grandma tries to act like them, too, and it's absolute alien bullshit. I wonder if Oathpark has always been in this foggy state or if the accident caused everyone to change. I don't think about it too much anymore because I know I won't get much of an explanation out of anyone. It used to frustrate me but I've learned to move on at this point.

The warm weather in the summer seems to make the town worse. Everyone is around each other even more, fabricating their happiness in the water and airconditioned candy shops. Grandma has more visitors. Grandpa works at the shop but at least he rarely brings anybody home with him. Some of Grandma's friends I actually don't mind; mainly because they bring food over ninety-nine percent of the time. They are Georgia-peach housewives, still, and I don't like it.

People in school aren't all that bad, surprisingly. There are obvious complications for me, but it's actually nice when people choose to stay away from you because they think you're a blind weirdo.

The students and teachers all have the same cloud over them, though. I can tell by their airy voices and expectations. That's what everyone seems to live for in Oathpark: beating expectations and wishing. Walking down the roads, the feeling of the pavement under my feet, is odd sometimes because I can feel the exhaustion of the cracks that no one seems to fill. The people of

Oathpark are exactly like its own streetways: there are so many cracks yet everyone keeps walking on them and ignoring the damage that the pavement has endured.

Anything that takes me away from reality I try to consume as much as possible. My dreams take me away from reality. Music takes me away from reality. Ryker takes me away from reality. The true reality of this town doesn't exist, so I continuously create my own away from its gravel matter. Growing up with Oathpark and my dreams, I've realized that Oathpark is its own dream and it holds multiple nightmares that I don't know about.

One day I'll be able to find out all of the nightmares and daydreams that everyone lives by and break this cloud that everyone walks under.

The most ironic thing about this town is that I can't see; yet I see clearly through all of the games. I see through that same cloud; the illusion of success that has never existed.

People of Oathpark are blind to their own realities while I continue to discover mine. I hope things change, but I can't tell if they'll be for the better or for the worse. I can feel the change; and it is coming like a dream.

HANA FERGUSON

Chapter Three

The dreamless night makes me wake up with an uneasy feeling. I try to tell myself that it is just one dreamless night; that is isn't a big deal. But my conscience seems to only have one answer: *So what, you skipped a dream! At least you didn't skip a period.*

I try to completely ignore it and get dressed as usual and have breakfast as usual and listen to music as usual. I try to do everything 'as usual' today and it seems to keep me distracted but I still have a strange feeling. I don't like it.

I'm rolling balls of packaged cookie dough between my palms to bake when I hear a knock at the door. "Oh, boy," I mumble under my breath as Grandma says that if it is yet another police officer she will have to put *me* under investigation. I roll my eyes and go back to rolling the sticky dough while she answers the door.

"Oh, Ryker, come on in," I hear Grandma say and Ryker's boots clank against the wooden floor. He must have just got back from working at the shop.

"Hey, Denise, really lovin' those flowers out there. The puppy garden statue is a cute touch." What a charmer.

"Thank you, dear. Orchid helped me."

I hear his boots clank over to me as I'm rolling a smaller hunk of dough. I can smell his cologne and the earthy undertones of his clothes from being outside.

"Better save me one of those cookie dough balls, *Poppin' Fresh*," he quotes me as I chuckle and hand him a cookie dough ball. I pop them in the oven and wash my hands.

"Was that all you came for?" I ask as I dry my hands. His mouth is still full of cookie dough as he answers. "Psh, no . . . I was wondering if you wanted to take a walk with me."

"Sure, just let me get my shoes on. Grandma, can you take care of those cookies?" "You bet, peach," she likes using cute fruity nicknames. It is another one of those additives to Things to Put in Your Grandma's Book of Sayings. I think by now we could publish a few.

I slip my shoes on and feel for my umbrella, but Ryker tells me to leave it.

What? "Why? You know I'll ne—"

"No, you only think you need it. You can make your

way around just fine," he is being stern so I drop it defensively and feel it land at my feet. The presence of Grandma and Grandpa's eyes on me. They don't intervene. They probably agree with Ryker and I don't blame them.

I grab his arm hesitantly as we walk out the door and the humidity greets me instantly. I feel thick grass underneath my feet for a few seconds until we get onto the pavement and walking is a lot more comfortable. It is silent besides young birds chirping, I can feel the warm sun slightly fading, figuring it is near evening. This reminds me of the first time I tried going on a walk by myself since I became blind.

I was barely fourteen, a rainy week in April and Grandma and Grandpa were in the field behind our house talking to one of our neighbors about a storm that was starting to brew. I wanted to do something on my own for once and figured it would just be a very short walk. I slipped out without them noticing, and pranced down the street, feeling rebellious for once in my life. As I kicked my sandals off and carried them in my hands, muggy air and slightly strong wind whipped my hair, and I'll never forget the feeling of invincibility I gained from walking down an empty road alone.

The wind got stronger though as I moved my

way through gravel and the smell of damp asphalt tickled my nose as warm raindrops kissed my face. I stopped, a rock stuck in between my big toe, and draped my arms out like a bird's weightless wings. Freedom flowed through my veins, my body as light as a feather, and my head deep into an abyss of clouds.

The rain began to pound on my skin harder, its soft drops turning into vigorous streaks along my face and hair. I spun around, my cheeks hurting from smiling so wide with joy . . . until Grandma's shrieking nestled itself against my ear. I turned around, the feeling of her hand bruising my arm never leaving my senses and the sound of rain from that day engraving itself into my heart.

"So, where exactly are we going?" I ask Ryker, curiosity shaking me from my thoughts.

"We should stop by Oathpark's nature preserve and sit by the lake. I needed to get out of the house, Mom was ready to kick me out on the porch for the rest of the day if I *didn't get off my ass with my guitar and actually go do something with my summer*," he mocks.

"Oh. Well, you're definitely off your ass and there is still plenty of summer left."

"Yeah, but I think you know what my mom meant."

"If I do, I'll make sure to let you know. . . ." I reply, sort of uncertain, as the arm I linked with Ryker's begins to sweat.

"Oh come on, Orchid," he says. Oh, God. He *rarely* uses my full name. "I heard you guys talking in the basement when Carson called. The call only lasted thirty seconds but your guys' shit-gossip about me lasted a good five minutes." he doesn't sound serious but there is a type of bitterness in his tone.

"We were only talking about the guitar riff-off contest and Christine brought up some other stuff, I guess." "I'm not upset. I just heard the conversation about how mom claimed I basically wasn't treating you the same as everyone else. I just feel bad, because I think she was right about that. The *summer* she was referring to was *you*. You're my summer."

I feel a slight blush blister my cheeks. "So that was what the whole *'you don't need your umbrella anymore'* hogwash was for? You're kidding me. That's it, I'm going back for the umbrella, and not because I think I need it, but because I think you're an asshole." I start to turn back to my house and Ryker grabs my arm and starts laughing. His laugh cracks with summer sweetness and charisma and I can't help but laugh, too.

"No, I really do think you shouldn't carry that old thing anymore. Sometimes change is good."

As he says that, it immediately reminds me of how I didn't dream at all last night. A pit falls deep into my stomach as we continue walking. I try to focus on my footsteps and the birds instead of the unwavering anxiety that flutters throughout my stomach and up my throat. It doesn't help much either way because the birds are anxiety with wings. It feels like they are all flying around me abruptly, chirping and screeching in my ears. All four of my senses are acting all at once and not being able to see anything makes the overload a whole lot more suffocating.

The muggy smell of Oathpark's lake brings me back to my *actual* senses as I feel the grass curl underneath my feet. I hear the water calmly slosh back and forth and it suddenly reminds me of the sound of the water from my dream; except that everything was numb then.

It makes me appreciate having Ryker here to enjoy it with me.

We find a bench to sit on and I begin thinking about Officer Dean's late night visit last night and my Grandma's secretive whispering. I wonder if the guy they were talking about was on the news and that possibly Ryker heard of him, too.

THE SOUND OF RAIN

"Officer Dean came by last night," I say as a few children laugh behind us.

"I bet your Grandma was happy then, but I think your Grandpa would beg to differ." he jokes.

"Yeah, yeah. Well, they discussed something rather strange. . . ," I trail off, trying to find a better way to bring it up. I realize that the only information I have is based off of what I heard from their gossip in the living room. "It was about a man. Grandma sounded really upset." "I'm not sure. Maybe my mom knows about it," he says. *Does Ryker sound uncomfortable?*

"He showed them a picture of the man and I really wanted to see it."

"Maybe it was best if you didn't. Mugshots aren't cute, you know. Could have been a picture not even his own parents would want for their wallets."

Ryker makes me laugh; all of the time. And by doing that, I know different points of his humor, whether it be dry or satire, and how he uses it. In this case, he's using it to stall. I can feel that he is hiding something.

"I'm pretty sure it wouldn't be hard for our police department to catch him. You can't go too far in this town," he says. We are quiet for a while, just listening to the waves crashing against the dock. I decide to drop the subject completely, not wanting to ruin the peace.

After a while, we get up and walk along the bike path, and walk back into town into Blu's Burgers— which is right next to Daisy Doughnuts—and grab something to eat. It is fairly quiet, besides Fleetwood Mac playing on the radio, as we sit at bar stools eating burgers and fries.

And besides Carson—very conveniently—showing up.

"Ryker, my man!" Carson's voice rings against my ears and his high-dollar cologne invades my senses. He has a few other guys of whom I don't know with him, too. I scoot my stool away a bit.

"Hey, bro," Ryker says with a mouthful of fries. I hear them do their signature handshake. I hope Ryker got grease on him.

"Ah, now who is she?"

I nearly choke on my burger as the background guys chuckle at Carson's remark. My face is red hot as I keep my head down, Ryker answering him, sort of stern.

"This is Orchid," I could feel him gesturing towards me. "She's my friend. She's coming with me on Friday to your party."

I'm suddenly reconsidering.

"Sweet," I can feel Carson's chest nearly touching my back as he inches forward and I can smell cigarette smoke mixed with his musky cologne. I hear Ryker stand up to take his tray, presumably to steer Carson physically away from me.

Yep, the reconsideration is strong.

I tune out their side-convo about the party and the guitar riff-off coming up soon for another guy on the other side of the burger bar talking to one of the waiters about the man from Georgia. It's basically the same type of descriptions and warnings Officer Dean gave us, but when he begins describing what the man looks like, that is what really caught my ears.

"Yeah, he has dark brown hair and green eyes. . . ," I grabbed bits and pieces past the music. "Apparently he killed a few people who were related to him but no one has talked about it in years. One of the daughters is still around somewhere on the map, all grown up now," Interesting.

I got sucked out of that convo and back into Ryker and Carson's when his posse and him said their goodbyes.

"See ya, sweets," Carson snickers at me. I give him a stiff smile and I can feel the disgust radiating off of Ryker's body.

"Don't worry about him, he only acts like that in front of his dumbass friends." "It's okay," I reply.

Ryker's arm brushes against mine and it makes me forget all about Carson.

We have a quick milkshake for dessert and begin to walk back home. The air cooled down while we were inside and some of the humidity was drawn out, indicating nighttime. My body is calm as we walk, but my mind is racing with all of the information and happenings that have been popping up suddenly. A random man that nobody will tell me about is in our town, I don't have a dream for the first time in years, Ryker's nuisance friend hits on me (which, for the record, never happens in the first place) . . . what else?

The air changes as we walk further and I smell something odd.

"What are we walking near, Ryker?"

"Oathpark's cemetery,"

"Oh. Is it big?"

"Barely. There are only seventeen graves in it, and most of them date well before the nineteen-hundreds. The newest one is from nineteen-sixty-six."

"Interesting." I try and ignore the feeling.

I don't have the energy to talk, but as we get near my house, we stop and sit for a few extra minutes to rest and end up briefly chatting about memories of when I could see.

"I remember you with a head-full of brown hair," I say, chuckling and reaching up to his head to mess it up for emphasis. It is soft. "It was parted down the middle and you always had a leaf or two in it."

"Yep, still the same. Just cleaner, I suppose, now."

"You had the bluest eyes. I slightly remember being jealous of them. And you had a really cute nose,"

I feel him shift on the bench and the only noise that floats through the night air is the soft buzzing of crickets. "My nose is bigger now. Like a Muppet's nose," he jokes. I move my hand down to his nose and shake my head, disagreeing. I could feel a tiny sliver of skin dipping into the side of it.

"It has a scar," I furrow my brows as I feel underneath his nose and above his lip. Another rough dip. "Where did you get these scars from?"

"I don't remember, to be honest. It was a long time ago, though. Probably got them from messing around as a kid. They're nearly faded," his breath is warm on my hand and it sounds hesitant as he replies. I ignore the gesture as I move my hand up to his cheek; his cheekbones are sharp and so is his jawline.

"It feels like you have changed a lot but I still picture the little Ryker that you used to be," I say quietly, suddenly sad. "I wish I could see how much you have changed physically. Your personality is still the same. Still the best."

I move my hand down to his lips and they are smiling.

"I'm not trying to cover up or say that I am ugly or anything, but looks don't matter," he says. I smile and nod in agreement. I feel his hand reach up to mine on his face.

"It is just nice to see how humans change physically. I've only seen my childhood. I barely remember my childhood. I see none of my teenage years; and soon, none of my adult years. I wonder how much I have physically changed myself," I say. I knew what I look like partially already but the dreams are notorious for playing tricks. The physical appearance I was used to seeing in the dreams are just memories but mixed with unrealistic scenarios that have altered how I view them.

He snorts. "Still the scrawny strawberry blond I always see," I punch his arm. "Of course you have changed physically. You probably feel it all the time, with your mightier senses and all."

"I suppose. Physically, I feel normal. But I don't know what normal looks like . . . and I want to know."

"You're a curious cat, Orchid. I don't blame you. The one thing that you are not, though, is normal. Trust me," he chuckles and kisses the palm of my hand that is still above his lips. I lay my thumb on the side of his cheek. "You're anything but."

****

Later that night after Ryker walks me the rest of the way home, I fall right into bed. I want to fall asleep as soon as possible to make sure that my dreams aren't broken. I need to dream and if I don't, I'm going to be even more worried than I already am.

This is my world; and what am I to do without a

world? Especially one of my own where I have my own senses apart from everyone else's. I am always apart from everyone else.

HANA FERGUSON

Chapter Four

The next morning, I wake up in a frustrated daze. I didn't dream at all last night. I can't think of any reason as to why I suddenly stopped dreaming. I lay there in bed, hoping to try and fall back asleep again, but Grandma barges in and makes me get up. She claims it is half past noon.

After forcing myself out of bed and putting somewhat of an effort into getting dressed, I figure I'd go out into the garden. I feel the umbrella near my bed, but I don't feel the normal urge to grab it. I leave it there and walk out my bedroom door.

I trudge through the kitchen door, as the summer air greets me, suffocating me in humidity and heat. I sigh and hear slight giggles of children and grumbling lawn mowers a few blocks away, the smell of fresh-cut grass floating throughout the heavy air. There isn't much of a breeze.

I make my way carefully down the porch steps and keep walking straight until the grass underneath my Converse start to fade into lumpy patches of hard dirt and roots, indicating the base of the garden and the beginning of the dehydrated field.

I wipe my forehead continuously as I yank and pull weeds. I feel that there aren't as many flowers in that part of the garden than there are weeds; they are itchy against my hands as I pull them. At least the sweat that covers my hands provide a natural barrier on my raw palms.

After a while, Grandma comes out with a pitcher of lemonade and a plate of eggless cookie dough truffles and cheese sandwiches. I wash my hands with the hose and make my way over to the picnic table, the cool shade instantly changing my skin's temperature by what feels like at least ten degrees. I sit down and I can hear Grandma chewing a truffle across from me. I also smell cigarette smoke.

The lemonade is ice-cold and tart as the perspiration from the glass drips from my lips as I drink. The truffles are chilled and soft, the cookie dough chunky with rich chocolate chips. The sandwiches are also chilled and rich with sharp cheddar cheese and whole grain bread. We quietly sit and eat. I'm not really in the mood for talking, anyways.

I want to tell someone about what is happening to me so very badly. That is all I can think about. When I first started to have dreams, everyone mistook it as a joke. Or completely ignored it. Either way, both reactions made me bottle up my dreams and hush them away from reality.

Two glasses of lemonade, a thick sandwich, and three truffles later, Grandma thanks me for helping her and goes back inside. She tells me that her and Grandpa are going to the market in town and that they'll be back in time for dinner.

The lawn mowers stopped for the day it seems, and I can still hear a few children playing; but other than that, it is just the rare gusts of wind that whisper against my hot ears.

I continue to pull weeds quietly, feeling the sweat drip from my forehead. I begin to think of the weeds as my dreams, full of frustration. The weeds are suddenly every single complication or worry I have had to deal with and I pull at them with anger. My face is burning from the hot summer sun and my hands are stinging from pulling.

They swarm my head—every problem I have—like a mad person's song and it is stuck in rhythm with the weeds as I yank.

Mother, gone. . . .

Pull.

Grandparents hiding multiple things from me. . . .

Pull.

Being blind. . . .

Pull.

Officer Dean. . . .

Pull.

Ryker's dumb friends. . . .

Pull.

My dreams. . . .

I pull and rip at the weeds so hard, I fall back when one of the weeds come out of the ground. I pant, feeling a warm wetness around my eyes. I am hot and numb and I can't tell if they are tears or sweat. Every sound around me stops besides the ruffling of the dehydrated grass blowing lightly against the small gusts of humid wind. I also hear footsteps crunching in the grass.

I sit up quickly and listen. The individual is close. I can feel them.

I wipe my eyes with the bottom of my tank-top quickly and turn my body towards the footsteps. They are heavy footsteps and I figure that they are a male's. I don't recognize Grandma's, Grandpa's, or Ryker's footsteps. It is partially because of the grass crunching and overpowering the footstep itself. It is also because I don't recognize the shoe.

"Hello?" I call out, my voice shocking my ears for a second. It is clear but raspy with heat.

No answer.

My heart begins to pound as the footsteps stop. I turn my head around to try and catch any sound of human life around me. I can feel the individual watching me and it makes me squirm in my skin.

I stand up slowly, taking my surroundings into consideration so that I won't come in contact with the person. I brush dead grass and dirt off of my hands and stand there, turning my head slightly once again. The individual is standing fairly close to me; on my right side, to be specific. I can smell a faint scent of sour alcohol and the cleanliness of soap—the person's odor is strangely familiar. I slide more to my left side to get further away.

I hear a metal *clink* and the sizzling of a flame coming to life. It is followed by the scent of cigar smoke. I inch away even further, the back of my legs sticky with sweat as I stood there. I hear the individual cough and it is husky and deep, indicating that the individual is, in fact, a male as I suspected.

I imagine he is just lighting a cigar to taunt me and my senses.

"I have no clue who you are, but you can be arrested for coming on my property," I manage to say. He doesn't answer. I keep slowly moving towards the back door, crushing a couple of flowers in the process. I don't want to provoke the man. I can tell that he hasn't moved. I figure that if he really wanted to hurt me, he would have done it already, but I still keep my guard up.

I hear his footsteps begin to crunch again and I begin to move a little quicker towards the door. I stand at the porch and realize he is walking through Grandma's rose bushes, which leads out of the yard. He is leaving.

I run inside, the air conditioning almost immediately freezing the sweat dripping off of my body. I pant and feel for the locks on both of the doors and lock them quickly. I feel nauseous while doing so and I stumble over to the front door, attempting not to puke my guts out, and lock that one, too. I make sure everything is locked.

I go over to the kitchen sink and wash my hands and face with ice cold water and soap. I scrub dirt from my fingernails, but the dirt is really deep into the creases of my nails so I clean them as best as I can feel. The soap slightly stings my palms and face.

When I'm finished, I feel a little better. I figure I have a sunburn because my arms and face feel hot and sensitive to the touch. I grab a bottle of water from the fridge —I can tell by the little bumps of design on top of the bottle that it's Dasani—and try to make my way into the living room, but my balance is off. A cold, hard surface greets my cheek painfully as I topple over. My head begins to throb right along with my heart and I mentally know that I'd fallen and that I should get up but I physically can't. I decide to lay there on the cool floor.

I clumsily open my bottle of water, it's coolness dripping down my raw palms, and chug it. It drips down my chin and neck and it soothes some of the burning. I close the water bottle as best as I'm able to and lay it next to me, and before I know it, I'm out.

****

I can't feel anything—I feel numb. The sunburn is gone. I can feel myself still lying down.

Am I asleep yet?

Am I dreaming now?

Am I awake?

My mind is racing and all I see is the usual

blackness I always see; but I have lost touch with reality while I sit in the deep darkness of my own mind. It is terrifying me; and it knows.

Whoever—whatever—is watching me, right now, knows.

I still feel numb, except I can feel waves of floating water underneath me. They're thick tides, as thick as molasses. They're slow and taunting—they grow along with my anxiety.

I feel eyes on me, even though I cannot look back at them. Still the same blackness I always see, and if this is a dream, none of the normal vibrancies I usually witness are here.

I can still move, turn my head side to side, curl my fingers—just as I usually would . . . but the tension is floating along my body with the molasses river and I don't want to move.

I turn my head slightly regardless of my thoughts and a screaming mouth flashes right in my face—the blood dripping from its lips is deep and gruesome. It keeps flashing, trying to push through the darkness beneath my eyelids as if it were a television program on a fuzzing screen trying to get through to connection. I keep staring in horror as I hear the mouth screaming, trying to get through to me.

The mouth's screams are feminine—they are as smooth as silk yet jagged as a knife to my ears. I can't move my arms to cover my ears, in fear I would miss something—it feels like I am in a trance. I'm not sure whether or not I want to wake up.

A male's deep scream pierces my ears, blending with the female's.

Screaming, fighting, crying: abuse.

The screaming fades into sobs for a few briefs seconds and then silence. The visual of the mouth floats away, almost glitching out of my eyes and then there is nothing.

There is nothing. . . .

"Nothing," I cry, but ironically nothing hears me.

It isn't long before I notice that I am not floating anymore. I'm falling. The numbness is receding and I can feel my stomach drop as I fall—there is nothing euphoric about it. My senses are stronger now and everything around me feels suffocating—all I see is black, but the strength of my senses makes spots of color gather underneath my eyes and I am sure my head is going to explode.

I can hear, feel, smell, and taste every individual wisp of wind that twirls around me, every white noise that isn't really there. Vibrations buzz in my chest; it feels like my veins are pulsing above my skin instead of beneath it.

The tears that pour out of my eyes and drip on my

cheeks are scorching hot and it feels like someone is pouring lava on me. My body heat is rising despite the wind and I pick and scratch at my arms in pain, trying to scream, but nothing comes out.

I am hot and hopeless and there is no one here, falling with me, to save me.

If this is what dying is like, I don't want to. I can't.

I can't. . . .

I can't.

As I fall further, I grow hotter, and feel hands. They are grabbing at my arms and legs, and shaking me. I swear they are chanting my name; their voices crumbling with static and screeches.

"Orchid,"

"Orchiddd,"

"Orch—"

"Orchid,"

I gasp as I feel a hand on my forehead and another one shaking me slightly on my arm. The slight burning sensation is still there and I wince at the physical contact. I groan.

"Oh, thank God," I hear Grandma's voice. It is shrill

against the nausea I'm feeling. "Are you hurt? You are burning up! Jesus, how long were you outside for?"

"O-out?" I croak. My throat hurts.

I swat her hands away, not to get rid of her, but to get her natural body heat away from me. All of the touching is making me feel worse.

"Yes, out. Outside. You were pulling weeds when I left. I should have never left you out there alone in this heat. I think I should call an ambulance,"

Oh, God. It was just a dream. More like a nightmare, rather.

I shake my head. " N-no . . .oh, yeah. Pulling . . . weeds. .
. ." I say slowly, still in a haze.

She checks my forehead again. She probably thinks that I took some acid or something. I know for a fact that I sound bonkers; doubtless that I look it, too.

"I think you might have sun poisoning. Come on, let's get you in a cold bath," she says, pulling my arms up. I eventually come to my senses and try to stand up without puking all over her.

We make our way to the bathroom and shut the door behind us. I sit on top of the closed toilet and rub my eyes, the burnt skin around them sensitive. I hear Grandma turn the bathtub faucet on. I begin to peel off my damp tank-top that is soaked with sweat. Grandma helps me get my pants off since they are completely stuck to me and my muscles don't have the energy for me to use them to pry them off.

Once the bath is done running, I step in, the smell of vinegar greeting me.

Yuck. Vinegar baths for sunburns.

While cold vinegar and water baths work, they still stink. I crinkle my burnt nose.

The cool water rises a couple of inches above my ankles as I step in. I sit down slowly, gasping lightly with pain and relief from the cool water floating beneath me.

Floating.

I sit up quickly and feel for Grandma's arm. My heart begins to beat with the remembrance of my dream. "I'm right here, honey," she says as she touches my face gently with a cool washcloth. I close my eyes as she softly scrubs, trying not to irritate my skin.

After a little while of awkward silence and scrubbing, I sit back and remember the man that came in our yard when I was pulling weeds. I must have a strange look on my face because Grandma asks me what the matter was. I'm contemplating on telling her everything, but decide against it.

"Nothing," I say, running my hands against the bottom of the tub and lifting my knees to my chin. "The vinegar is making my nose burn."

****

After the cold bath, I get dressed in one of my thin silk nightgowns, since every other fabric irritates my skin right now, and lie down in my room, removing the thick comforter from my bed and leaving only the cool sheets to cover up with. The bath made me feel better but I still feel sick and I can't get the uneasy feeling out of my scalded system. I feel sensitive to everything.

Grandma comes in and places an ice cold bowl in my lap.

"Chocolate ice cream," she says. "Eat."

I start to take small bites of the rich ice cream, but the sweetness is strong against my taste buds, beginning to make me nauseous again. I hear a bottle open and Grandma gently rubs some aloe vera on my face, neck, shoulders, and arms. It smells sweet and earthy and it's soothing on my throbbing skin. I hear her shake a small bottle and she grabs my hand gently, dropping a small pill in it.

"Ibuprofen."

I take the ibuprofen and chug some water, the cold liquid lubricating my sore throat.

Grandma kisses the top of my head.

"Thank you, Grandma." I say.

"No need to thank me, Orchid." she replies as I feel the bed shift and hear the door open, revealing Grandpa's sing-song voice.

I lay my head against my pillow and close my eyes, taking a deep breath, listening to Grandpa's distant singing of Carl Smith's *I Overlooked an Orchid*.

I must have fallen asleep again, but not for long. There were no dreams. There were no nightmares. Just blackness. I'm startled awake by a strong hand touching my hair and I flinch, my heart pounding out of my chest, and quickly grip the hand. I pull back when a voice shouts.

"Orchid! Orchid, Jesus, it's alright," he claims. I sigh a relieved breath, realizing it's Ryker. I let go of his hand, leaning back. My breathing is really heavy and my chest hurts. I suddenly have the urge to cry; I'm getting sick of being frightened so much in less than a twenty-four-hour period. I bet it hasn't even been five hours.

I cover my face, embarrassed. I feel tears prick my eyes heavily and my face contort and strain, ready to blubber. "Orchid, I'm sorry, I didn't mean to scare you." Ryker whispers and pulls me to him. I shake my head and let out a small sob. I hug him back briefly, his shirt scratching lightly against my sunburn. He smells like he just got back from the shop but I like it.

"It's okay, it isn't you," I manage to say after I'm done. I wish humans could choose whether or not they wanted to cry at a certain moment. That could have been me blubbering right there, in front of a crowded room, if anyone else were to show up. *Don't jinx it.*

"You smell like pickles."

I chuckle and wipe my nose. "Grandma's home remedy for sunburn. I'm a burnt pickle now."

"Ah, well it looks like it worked. The redness isn't all that bad."

When he mentions the color red I immediately think of the bright crimson beets Grandpa grew and pickled in jars when I was little. I hope I'm not that red.

"Did Grandma let you in?"

"Yeah, I just figured I'd stop by after work. Your grandpa stopped by the shop for a bottle of motor oil and told me what happened. They both are out in the garage right now."

Ryker's dad owned the shop for the longest time before he passed away. It was an organized place, although there was always some sort of grease stain somewhere, from what I've heard. Christine never really talks about his dad.

I wipe my nose. "Can I tell you something?" I ask. This is it. I can't take the weight on my chest anymore. I have to say something.

"Of course."

"I have a couple of things, actually. But you have to promise me you won't say anything. It's really important that you don't, because I'm trying to figure this out on my own."

"Okay. Shoot."

"My dreams have stopped suddenly," I say There is a stillness in the room. I haven't mentioned the dreams occurring in years and although Ryker and I are close, having this feeling of sudden insecurity and fear is strange. I'm afraid he'll brush them off again like he did when he was younger; but I also think that he has matured a lot over the years.

His voice broke into my thoughts. "*The* dreams?"

"Yes, *the* dreams. And nightmares, too. I haven't had one of *the* dreams in quite some time; they suddenly stopped. Earlier today when I passed out, it seemed like a dream was trying to come through, but it was more like a nightmare. It was really disturbing."

"What do you mean it didn't come completely through?" "No . . . it was coming in all unclear and staticky. The girl, she disappeared. She looks like me except the features are more emphasized and through our own different qualities." it feels weird saying *our* as if she is real.

"So you know what you look like now, technically?"

"Sorta. I think my dreams are a few years behind, though, unless I still look like a twelve year old girl." "Not at all," he chuckles.

"I have another thing or two to mention," I say, sitting up a bit more. I feel my head sink down with fatigue. I don't want to mention anything while I'm in this emotionally tired state but I know nothing will get fixed if I don't.

"A person was here earlier."

"Inside the house?"

"No, when I was out gardening. They were standing near me and watching me. I'm pretty positive it was a man," I say. My heart is beating so hard I think it'll pop right out of my chest. "It was like he was taunting me. And as he got closer, the scent of him was so familiar."

"Did he touch you? Did he say anything?" the edge on his voice startles me.

I shake my head and hear him sigh.

"I'll come over every single day from now on and try to be with you whenever I can," he says. I grasp his arm and pat it affectionately, despite the annoyance of him being over-protective. "Do your grandparents know?" I shake my head again.

"You need to tell them," he says sternly. I can feel my sudden frustration flow slowly throughout my whole body.

"I've told you this because there is something definitely wrong with me and I thought you would help me," I exclaim. "I never tell anyone anything related—even the least—to my dreams, Ryker, because nobody understands! And I'm starting to think you *still* don't understand. You can't tell anyone what I've told you. If you do Ryker, I swear to Go—" a loud pound on my study desk interrupts me. *"Goddammit*, Orchid!"

I shut up immediately. Ryker lowers his voice. "I do understand. You can't keep this from your grandparents, especially if there is some fucking creep roaming around here waiting to attack. I'm sorry for not understanding when we were kids, but it's time to move on. I swear to God Orchid, if you allow whoever that was come near here again and something bad happens, I won't blame you. I'll blame myself. You expect me not to do anything after you tell me this?" his rhetorical question oozes with frustration.

I sit in silence, stunned.

After a few long moments of silence, I lie back down slowly and turn, my back facing him.

His eyes are on me. They are disappointed.

THE SOUND OF RAIN

Chapter Five

Visits at multiple different optometrists and therapists and other specific eye doctors whose professional titles are too hard to pronounce throughout my childhood have always ended with the same disappointing outcome: nothing can be proven and nothing can be done. The usual cases were that I'm either imagining things or that my mental health is so weak that it is causing me to have manifestations of things I last saw before I became blind. I stopped going to every single medical professional I was assigned to due to their lack of actual answers when I was thirteen. I remember an interesting visit with a therapist when I was twelve.

Grandma and I were sitting in Dr. Rupert Parish's office in a plush leather couch next to each other. The room smelled of ivory soap and carpet cleaner and Grandma complained quietly that he always used way too much air freshener and that he should open a window for once. I bent my legs underneath me so that I was sitting Indian-style and felt on the table beside me for a magazine. Some of the magazines had taped lines of Braille describing what outfits that the models were wearing that Dr. Parish stuck on the magazines himself. I picked up a Seventeen magazine and flipped through it, feeling the descriptions of the outfit on the cover, wishing that I could see the assigned clothing and the implied beautiful model that represented them. One of the descriptions read: *"Beautiful young woman with glowing skin and very long, peachy-blond hair. A very wide, bright smile creases against her plush cheeks."*

I smiled at the description. He notices a lot. Maybe too much.

His footsteps interrupted my euphoria and I laid the magazine back on the table next to me. I could smell his cologne across from me and it was strong. I could imagine Grandma scrunching her nose with disapproval.

"Hi, Orchid." he greeted.

"Hello," I replied.

"Hello, Mrs. Dahl."

"Hi, Dr. Parish."

Greetings were always short and simple. I think I'd only heard Grandma say something else to him besides a greeting once, and that was to give him paperwork information for when we had started the trials. That was going to change, though.

I heard him scribble something on his notepad

before becoming settled in the seat again. He was a very kind yet sort of awkward individual. He knew at times when he paused that he made you feel awkward but he never cared. I had gotten used to it after a few visits.

"Are your dreams still occurring?" he asked. His voice was deep yet light with genuine concern. He asked me this at every. Single. Visit.

I shrugged. "They occur all the time. I can't remember all of them, though, like with normal dreams. They come and go. There are very odd ones and there are very vague ones. But the ones that bother me most of all are the ones that have a girl that looks just like me in them." I explained. I could hear more scribbling on his notepad. He sighed.

"How do you know she is you? You haven't seen yourself in five years. You grow with age and your features look much older now. You don't look the same as you were when you were seven," Dr. Parish reminded me. His voice was hard on the questions but he wasn't being rude.

"I know this already," I stated. "But I just *feel* it. I *feel* her. She is me. I am her. Nobody will understand this. Nobody has. There is a bond that I feel."

There was a long pause and the room was silent. I settled

my elbow on the arm of the chair and leaned the side of my head against my hand and waited for a reply. I felt Grandma shift uncomfortably next to me.

It wasn't until when Dr. Parish stood up and Grandma followed that *I* began to feel uncomfortable. As I heard their footsteps exit the room, I was in disbelief.

What are they doing?

I wanted to get up and pound my fists on the door but I sat anxiously and waited instead.

"Her condition is impossible," I heard Dr. Parish whisper fiercely. He whispered something else and Grandma replied but I can't make it out. It felt like hours before they finally returned into the room, Grandma's floral scent sitting along with her as she plopped back down next to me.

"What was that about?" I asked. I wanted *any* answer.

Dr. Parish cleared his throat and asked, to my amazement: "Does anyone else show up in your dreams?"

He's avoiding the question. Grandma never answers anything so I don't blame her. But he's a jerk for ignoring his twelve-year-old patient.

I paused, scratched my arm that itched with discomfort and anger, and moved in closer to his face in front of me. "I won't tell you unless you tell me." A long pause.

"I needed to ask your grandmother and evaluate a couple of questions that were on some paperwork she filled out for me, honey." he stated. He sounded the same when he lied. He must have been a pretty good liar to other people, but I could tell that he was lying through his teeth.

"Grandma, can you leave for a few moments?"

"Honey, I'm supposed to be in here,"

"It's okay. I just want to talk to Dr. Parish."

He's a doctor, after all.

I heard her footsteps slowly patter against the tile floors. They reminded me of loud ticks on a grandfather clock.

"You're lying." I stated, after Grandma had shut the door. I wasn't rude when I stated it as it was—a fact. "Orchid, I'm here to listen to *you.* You're not to listen to what I say about anything outside of our session, including paperwork."

"That wasn't paperwork."

"How do you know if it was paperwork or not? You weren't there when your grandmother and I were talking," he stated.

"Why are you always stating that about everything?" I exclaimed. "I heard you guys talking out there. My 'condition' is something that I may not know about but still deal with and I have a right to know."

"Because it's true," he exclaimed back. The thick crinkle of the leather seat accentuated his voice as he moved. "You were never there during the accident, Orchid. You were physically there, but mentally, you were gone. Adios. Done," he said as he made reality seem like a dream itself.

"You weren't mentally there for the accident, you weren't there for what I was discussing with your grandma. You need to understand that the little details that you think you know about your situation, you truly don't know."

What a *freaking* hypocrite.

"How would you know, then?"

"I don't, either, Orchid. There are people who do, though. People who should have told you. Your condition . . . it's something I have never seen before. I don't even think there is a name for it. The way you can control it is if you know, but I don't have the right to tell you."

I simply got up and walked my way quickly to the door. I couldn't believe what I was hearing. One minute he 'kind of' agrees with me and the next minute he tells me I don't know anything.

I ignored Grandma calling out my name and went straight to the car where I sat for at least fifteen minutes, completely alone. When Grandma came and sat down in the driver's seat, we sat for another five minutes as she smoked a cigarette. I was guessing she didn't know what to say or how to explain. She started the car eventually and we left. That was my last visit to any form of mental health specialist. I would probably beg to differ for Grandma.

****

Looking back at it, I was simply a whiny twelve year old, I think. I felt neglected and while I don't agree with whatever Grandma and Dr. Parish did, I still was bratty. I do know one thing, though, out of the whole situation that is absolutely true—if there is anything I hate the most, it is liars.

THE SOUND OF RAIN

HANA FERGUSON

<u>Chapter Six</u>

Grandpa and I are sitting in a booth at the automotive shop waiting for Archie, Ryker's uncle who owns the shop now, to finish dealing with a customer. The automotive shop is half car repair and shop and half gas station and pit-stop. Grandpa dragged me with because I had a choice of either going with him for the day or going with Grandma to a Mary Kay cosmetic party. My choice was rather obvious.

Despite Ryker still being pissed at me, he is here, stacking boxes of car parts in the shed on the side of the shop. We greeted each other when Grandpa and I arrived and he asked me how my sunburn was doing. I told him it was feeling better and that was it. He'll get over it eventually, I figure—I have my reasons for not telling my grandparents everything. I can't make them be on edge all of the time just because of one incident. Stupid, I know. Petty, even . . . but there are plenty of things Ryker never tells Christine about when I think he should.

Anyways, he can't stay mad at me forever.

I hear thick, hard stomps towards Grandpa and I notice a strong breeze of table cleaner waft underneath my nose and a squeaky, scrubbing sound moving along the table, causing it to shake.

"Pretty good weather, Gerry, huh?" a deep, thick Southern accent greets us.

"Yeah Archie, if humidity as thick as butter is your liking," Grandpa retorts.

"The thicker, the better. Good workin' weather. Hey there, Orchid Petal. How's summer treatin' you, sweetie?" the table stopped shaking and I heard Archie set the spray bottle down.

"Decent." I reply with a complete lie. Decent, for now, sure—but as far as everything else . . . not a drop of decency so far.

"Good, good. If you ever want a summer job moving stuff, we got an open position."

"Don't be putting that kind of work off on my granddaughter, Archie," Grandpa barges in.

"What? Just offering. I wouldn't think she'd want it anyway. Her and Ryker are constantly around each other in general, imagine them twenty-four-seven here," Archie exclaims with a hearty laugh. I force a laugh, too, all while my cheeks feel like two forest fires blazing on the sides of my face.

"Aw, leave the sweet girl alone, Arch," a soft,

feminine voice chastises. "She's too pretty to be doing labor."

"I'm *joking,* Darla," Archie chuckles. "Laugh for once, would'ja?"

"I do laugh!" Darla giggles. Darla works as a cashier for the pit-stop part of the shop. Her and Archie have the hots for each other but they don't really go through with their actual feelings besides flirting.

"You should do it more, your smile is too beautiful to waste."

Darla giggles again at Archie's comment and I hear her heels click away from the table.

Grandpa and Archie go back to talking about the shop and it's business as I sit and force myself to listen to the low radio music playing. It's some classic rock station that circulates only five decent rock songs, mostly by Creedence Clearwater Revival and The Rolling Stones. Out of all of the bands I listen to, I'd have to say The Rolling Stones are my favorite.

A sharp *pssst* pulls me from the music.

I whip my head around, hoping the whisper will somehow make itself clear again.

"Come help me," Ryker's voice amplifies against

my ear, making me jump.

"Jeez," I reply, putting a hand up to my chest. I feel a sharp corner nudge my other hand and I grab at it.

"Help me carry some boxes. These ones are lighter,"

The fact that everyone keeps underestimating my strength is beyond me.

I grab the box and stand up, following the clank and scuffles of his boots outside and against the concrete in front of me. We set the boxes down and I begin help him organize a box of bolts and screws. The only sound between us is the light swishing of the trees in the humid air. I can feel beads of sweat form on my forehead.

As I'm feeling for bigger bolts, Ryker's hand meets mine. It is rough and soft at the same time and a tad bit damp from perspiration. The veins that bulge from his knuckles are strong and strained from long days here in the shop.

"You shouldn't overwork yourself." I state quietly.

"I'm not."

I cup both of his hands in mine and rub them

lightly. "Your hands say otherwise."

He fits his fingers in through mine. "Are you a palm reader now?"

I laugh and shake my head. "Just reminding you to not be a perfectionist all of the time."

He sighs with agreement as he lets my hands go gently. "I'm still upset with you for not saying anything to your grandparents."

"If the guy wanted to hurt me truly, he could have easily done it the minute he started walking around my backyard. My 'mightier senses and all' actually work, you know," I reply with an edge.

"I don't care. If you don't tell them, I will."

I rip my hand out of the box. "That's not your dirty work to do. You shouldn't worry about it. It's been weeks since it happened. I'm trying to figure things out on my own and learn on my own and be my own person, but you're not allowing it, and it's pissing me off."

"It *is* my dirty work because you're not doing anything about it! A fucking psycho is running the streets here, specifically your backyard, and you're just dillydallying around,"

"Drop it, Ryker. I can take care of it myself. You

don't have to watch out for me all of the time." my head is whirling with memories of the garden scenario and Officer Dean and my grandparents. My state of mind is gone at the moment.

I turn to leave through the back of the shed door and I feel Ryker grab my shoulders. It isn't violent, but it's alarming. "Orchid, it's important that you tell them! You have to underst—"

I don't feel myself do it.

My hand stings as I pull it back from his cheek. His grip instantly leaves my shoulders, the pressure still there against my skin. I clutch the hand I slapped him with in my opposite palm, astonished, feeling it's foreign form.

I can't believe myself.

I've never hit Ryker. I've never hit anybody.

I back away towards the shed wall. The shed is quiet. I hear our breathing against the humid gusts of wind coming through the shed window. I swallow my spit. My mouth is dry as hell.

"I'm so sorr—" I try to say, but the pounding of his boots against the concrete floor and the slamming of the shed door interrupt me. I sit on the ground alone with

the box of bolts and screws and sort them with my shaking hands and try to act like my life is somewhat put together.

I feel so bad. Physically and mentally. And there isn't a thing I can do about it.

Grandpa and I leave the auto shop after a while and he drops me back off at the house and leaves again to go get Grandma. While we are in the car, I act like everything is fine. He tells me that they will bring dinner back home—Chinese food, courtesy of Grandma's close friend Lynn Wong at the cosmetic party—and that it shouldn't take long. I rush into my bedroom as soon as he drops me off and slam the door and scream into my pillow. I'm so frustrated with everything, including myself. I have lost a lot in my life . . . and now I'm sure I've lost my best friend.

A few moments after my screaming fit, I turn on my radio and *Everlong* by Foo Fighters jives through the speakers. I sit up and nod my head to the beat. It hurts and my cheeks are wet but I don't care. Nodding my head leads to moving my arms and eventually, I'm standing on top of my bed, moving my whole body, my mattress creaking with every step my feet take against the comforter. I blast the music up louder and jump on my bed as hard as I can and yank the pillows and chuck them against the wall.

It feels so good to let out all of this energy. This horrible fucking energy that I can't hold any longer.

I scream the main chorus during the guitar solo and my throat is raw from screaming into my pillow from before but I don't care. I hope people can hear me. I want someone to hear me for once in my life.

I wish I could tear everything apart in my bedroom and the house and the garden and this whole town that is clouded with a thick darkness of secrets and bullshit. I imagine the town in a long, black abyss after killing every single thing off and the night sky blazing with the flames I'd love to start, the stars numb little dots. Then, I imagine myself jumping in with the flames and killing off the catastrophe I call my life. I don't think I'd feel a thing. Not one little thing.

After the song ends, I turn the music down and I flop back on my bed, out of breath. I push myself underneath my tangled blankets and sheets, and fall asleep.

The next morning, I wake up with a bad mood, sore throat, and a headache. I go into the bathroom without saying good morning to Grandma and Grandpa and lock myself in there to take a shower.

I peel off all of my clothes and turn the water on. It flows against my body in scorching streams. The steam feels good in my aching throat and the water pounding on my head somewhat subsides the headache. As I rub my hands over my face, a flicker of an image of a man who is soaking wet with flames behind him manifests itself quickly behind my eyelids. I gasp and my eyelids shoot open. The silhouette of the man sits faintly against my black vision. I feel around the shower and make sure that I'm the only one in it.

I think I'm officially going nuts. I think I'm going to start accepting it.

I quickly scrub my whole body and hair and jump out of the shower and into my room as quickly as possible. I sit on my bed and feel in my nightstand for my Ibuprofen stash. I take two of them and lean back on my mattress. I sigh and rub my eyes to see if anything else would show itself behind my eyelids, but there is nothing.

After a few long moments of moping, I force myself up and get dressed into a T-shirt and some sweatpants. I don't plan on going anywhere at all today. I'm not in the mood.

I go into the kitchen and make some coffee.

Grandma is still sleeping, which is a shocker. Grandpa says hi to me from his living room chair.

"Want some coffee, Gramps?"

"I already had some, but it wouldn't hurt to have another."

I pour two mugs of coffee and carefully make my way into the living room. I sit on the couch and cover up with a blanket.

"Has anything been bothering you lately, Orca?" Grandpa asks.

I shake my head.

"I can tell when you're lying."

I lean my head back and respond with a groan.

"Tell me."

"Ryker and I are just arguing," I say. I mean to only say that, but something else blasts straight out of my ego, too. "And I'm sick of you and Grandma hiding things from me."

"We aren't hiding anything from you."

I turn my head towards his voice. "I can tell when you're lying."

He responds with a sigh. "Orchid, there is a lot that you need to know. But your Grandma needs to be here to talk about that with us, too. She needs to agree to tell you."

"Grandma isn't the only person in this house who is in charge. You are, too."

I hear him chuckle and cough after he sips his coffee. "Want to bet on that? We both know that I can't afford to tell you things we both haven't agreed on to tell you. We'd be digging my grave early."

I sip my coffee and drop the subject completely despite being pissed for not being told anything because I know he's right.

"I want you to remember something regarding you and Ryker's relationship," Grandpa says. I hear him shift in his chair. "Sometimes, life doesn't work out the way we want it to. We don't always do the right things or say the things people want to hear. We don't hear the things we want people to say. But we always end up, somehow, in the midst of being there for people even after not doing the right things all of the time. And the same goes vice-versa. And despite the mistakes that we all make, we all move on with time. Time is like a feather in the wind rubbing against your cheek—after it brushes your skin, you still feel the soft fibers of the feather tingle against your cheek, but you see it float away from you, far above you, until you can't ever see it again."

Around noon, I decide to call Ryker's house phone. I lean against the rough wall and fidget with the phone cord nervously. The rings are in sync with the pounds of my heart.

"Hello?" a female voice asks.

"Oh. Hey, Christine," I say.

"Hey, Orchid. How are you?"

"I'm alright, thanks for asking. Is Ryker home by chance?"

"He actually isn't right now. He's at the shop today working some extra hours with Archie. They're planning to do something big there, I guess. But I'll let him know you called when he gets home."

"Alright, thanks anyways."

"No problem. You should come over when you're not busy. We can have a girl's night or something soon."

"I'd like that," I smile. "Talk to you later, Christine."

"Bye, sweets."

I hang up the phone and trudge my way back to the couch. Grandma went to the store earlier after she woke up and Grandpa is snoring lightly in his chair. I decide to take a small nap, too. I have nothing better to do.

****

Grandma wakes us both up with veggie stir fry and brown rice for dinner. I realize that I never even ate anything today—besides drinking coffee and water before taking a nap with Grandpa. It smells so good and my mouth is watering. I scoop a heaping pile of it into a bowl and Grandma pours me a glass of milk. We all sit at the table, eating quietly.

"The sky isn't dark yet, is it?" I ask with a mouth-full of rice.

"Don't talk with your mouth full. It looks like a blooming bruised peach blossom in the sky."

After we all are finished eating, I help Grandma with the dishes and I go out into the backyard when it's cooler out. I sit on this old couch swing that Grandma has always had. It's pretty big, though, and I think the cushions need to be washed. But it's comfortable nonetheless.

I sit cross-legged and listen to the crickets chirping and the faint rumble of motorcycles in the distance. As I swing lightly, the air hits my fatigued face and ruffles my sweatpants a bit against my thighs. I feel much better than before, oddly enough. I think it's because I actually ate something and went outside for fresh air. I miss Ryker, still, though.

I count my blessings and the people around me. I love Grandma, even though it annoys me an exceptional amount that she won't tell me anything. I love Grandpa and his wise words. I love Christine because she is a mother figure to me.

And yes.

I love Ryker.

I love this town, despite its woes. I imagine the town burning in flames again underneath the tarnished navy sky, speckled with stars that cast a rusty-orange glow from the flames that wave beneath it. I never will hurt anything, though, in reality. Just the memories. The memories that I can't remember and the memories that I won't find out about. I will never hurt anything like anything hurts me. But I'm still thankful, because it makes me stronger, in a way. And with strength, I can be the fire that consumes and intimidates everyone else instead of watching it consume and intimidate me.

A shift on the swing startles me out of my thoughts. I gasp and jump up from the swing. A strong hand grabs my forearm.

"Relax," Ryker's voice illuminates in my ear loudly. My ears are numb to his voice specifically.

"Oh. Hi." I say as I sit back down.

"Hi."

"My mom told me you called."

"I did," I say. I pick at my nails in my lap. "I'm sorry."

"It's okay. I was being a pest. I was just trying to make sure that none of you were going to get, like, clobbered in the middle of the night or something." "Nothing has happened." I reply.

"Yet." Ryker states, matter-of-factly.

"Alright, Sheriff Einstein. I'm glad we are back to normal."

"I am, too."

I lift my hand up to his cheek. "I didn't whack

you too good, did I?" I scrunch my eyebrows with sympathy.

"No, you didn't." he replies quietly. I leave my hand there and I feel his face shift closer to mine. He smells like the shop's cleaner, fresh air, and faint laundry soap. I lean over and lightly kiss the cheek that I slapped. I don't realize it, but I let my lips travel down his cheek further until they're almost touching his lips . . . and he's kissing me.

When people say that you feel sparks and butterflies and hearts and crap flying all over the place while kissing someone—it's true. In fact, literally everything in the surrounding area stops, including time, yet everything on the inside of the human body just seems to be whipping around like a rollercoaster without its tracks. It's a crazy feeling, being kissed for the first time. Just saying.

I wrap my arms around his neck and he is warm. The air must have gotten colder while we've been out here because I'm freezing. But his body heat is welcoming and I try to take as much of it in as I can. His lips feel the same as I felt with my hands . . . soft and strong.

After a few long moments, we pull away and the connection instantly shuts off. I feel the strong energy that was raging through my veins drain completely and I lean against him. The feeling of his lips still linger against mine.

The bugs and crickets buzzing and chirping and the faint squeaking of the swing as we lightly swing back and forth are the only noises that consume our ears. Ryker breaks the silence with: "I wish you could see the amount of lightning bugs that are floating in your backyard right now."

"I wish, too," I whisper.

"They're all around us. A sea of flickering yellow that cascades us in the night."

"Lighting up a world that I yearn to see."

"You light up my world."

"Are you related to Shakespeare?"

"A hundred-percent not. That'd be pretty cool, though."

"It sure would." I say, hugging his warm side.

HANA FERGUSON

Chapter Seven

Growing up in school was difficult. Once I got into highschool, it surprisingly wasn't as bad as it was in middle school and grade school. I've got only one conclusion to my middle and grade school days: kids are really shitty. Like, beyond shitty. Ryker stuck up for me a lot throughout those days—thank God for him—so it was tolerable. I was in normal classes, I got around easy because everything had Braille on it, and the only time I ever needed a student aid was when I was in grade school when I was still getting used to my impairment.

I heard whispers often--about me, about my crazy dad. Never much about the accident because not many people knew exactly what happened. There was only talk about my dad; never about anyone else who might have been involved. There were rumors, though. And a lot of the kids never wanted anything to do with me, which looking back at it now, was kind of understandable. There were a lot of issues circling my life at the time. Being a dork probably didn't help much, either.

The grade school building was a few blocks from Ryker and I and we would walk to and from school together. It shut down a couple of years ago because of asbestos infecting the air; and now it sits alone on the corner of the street. Its abandoned foundation is a home for raccoons and, as rumored by my fellow classmates, ghosts. I wouldn't be surprised.

Ryker and I were walking home one day, our fifth grade year, and he was showing me his new portable CD player.

"This track is Lynyrd Skynyrd. Can you hear it?"

"Yes, Ryker, I'm blind, not deaf."

Ryker laughed and said: "Okay. Listen to the awesome guitar solo of *Free Bird*."

We shared headphones and I could feel his head bob up and down slightly. I giggled and told him to stop. I felt a shuffle near my feet and the side of the headphones that are on my ears ripped off of my head and I gasped.

Bike tires screeched behind us.

"Walking your little blind girlfriend home, Feldspar?" a satire voice taunted.

"She isn't my girlfriend. That was my brand new CD player, you better hope to God it isn't broken." Ryker sneered. We both stopped walking. I gripped the umbrella handle and Ryker's arm.

"Yeah, you're probably right. No one would want to date a blind person."

"That isn't true, Dunnell-dweeb." the kid who was taunting us was Kyle Dunnell. He never liked Ryker.

"I'll bet you twenty bucks that it is true,"

"I'm not betting your dumbass a dime."

"That means you don't have a dime to your name.
Blind Betty and Poor Paul sure do make a great couple!

"Get outta here," Ryker snapped.

"Make me."

Kyle Dunnell was something—a piece of work for sure. "Seriously, do you not have better things to do?" I asked.

"If you give me a kiss, I'll go away."

Ew. "Weren't you just making fun of me for being blind? It sucks for you because today is the day that you find out that even a blind girl wouldn't kiss you."

Ryker started chuckling; but as soon as he did, I heard a grunt and Ryker's arm ripped from my hand.

"Hey!" I shout. I felt a kick at my leg and both of them were yelling insults at each other. I bent and waved my hands around quickly until I felt an arm. I grabbed it and yanked it away as hard as I could. I fell backwards and the arm I grabbed was followed by a body toppling onto me.

"Get off of her," a deep voice echoed along the empty streets. I felt the sudden pressure pull up from my legs and stomach quickly. "Both of you boys will be in a lot of trouble. Harassing a young girl . . . not to mention, she's blind. Who's CD player?" that is something that will always be mentioned.

"Ryker wasn't harassing me, Officer Dean," I claimed. "Kyle was. Kyle was harassing both of us. Ryker was sticking up for me and I tried to break things up. None of this is Ryker's fault. Kyle broke Ryker's brand new CD player and it's worth a lot of money."

I heard Officer Dean sigh. "Kyle, go home. I'll be over at your house to talk to your parents. Ryker, grab your CD player and walk Orchid home, I'll be over to talk to your mom and your grandparents."

We both said goodbye and continued walking down the street.

"Thanks for sticking up for me, Ryker. Is it broken?"

"No, it's fine. Should I break it to make Kyle pay for a new one? And no need to thank me."

"Hmmm . . . that's kind of devilish. And there is," I

said. "You're the bestest friend a girl could ask for, Ryker Feldspar."

"A *blind* girl," Ryker stated.

"A label! Always a label." I nudged his shoulder and he put his arm around me.

"You're a pretty cool friend, too, Orchid Thomas."

"I like Lynyrd Skynyrd."

"I do, too."

We walked down the road and I remember feeling giddy. I was happy with being friends with just Ryker. He was the only true friend I've ever really had. He is the only true friend I *do* have. I don't think that will ever change.

HANA FERGUSON

Chapter Eight

The next morning—the day of the party I'm suppose to go to with Ryker—is hectic. I wake up (dreamless, once again) to Grandma and Grandpa arguing over something about the shop. I walk out of my room after I get dressed and into the kitchen, where I hear Grandpa sigh and Grandma zip her lips. Realizing they have stopped barking at each other because I've entered their premises, I silently make my way to the coffee cups in the cupboard near the sink and pour extremely hot coffee into one.

"You guys can still go about your business," I say.

"Just 'cause I'm in here doesn't mean you should quit discussing whatever needs to be discussed. I'm actually quite curious." I blow on the top of the mug. I can imagine Grandma's eyes rolling as hard as a rock skipping on the surface of a river as Grandpa wheezes with a chuckle.

"Your grandpa wants to help put in some sort of addition to the shop with Archie this weekend." she states. Grandma doesn't sound up for it. I shrug.

"What kind of addition?"

"A very large and heavy one," she scoffs. "Gerald, you're going to break your damn back!"

"You're breaking every damn marble and nerve I own right now, Denise."

I stifle a laugh. They argue but it's never on bad terms. Not *too* bad, at least.

"If Grandpa wants to help with whatever it is, you should let him help. There will be other guys there too if he needs help lifting something," I say.

Grandma sighs. "I don't care what you do, Gerald. Don't say I didn't warn you."

"Never warned me in that white dress of yours forty-two years ago and everything's just dandy." he's trying to butter her up. He makes me melt.

"What exactly is this addition, if I may ask again?"

"Ryker's uncle wants to add another section on the building for automotive repairing on cars," Grandpa replies. "All of his workers will be there, including Ryker."

"No siree, not tonight. Ryker is taking me to

a party at his friend Carson's house tonight."

"A party?" Grandma asks.

"We aren't even starting until tomorrow. Party?" Grandpa interrupts. I must have forgotten to mention it to them. Oops.

"Yes, a party," I say. They act like I don't have a life . . . I mean I get it, because my life isn't much, but I can still have *some* fun once in awhile . . . even if it means dragging an introvert into a colossal of social awkwardness and suspected drugs.

"My soapbox lectures and bible verses are reserved, young lady . . . and you're lucky I save them for church." Grandma's accent accentuates her threat.

Southern grandparents. Love 'em.

"So, that's a yes?"

"Yes, you can go. No in advance to whatever outfit you're trying on first." I roll my eyes. The first outfit chosen is always promiscuous it seems, but they seem to forget that I can't even see what I'm going to be wearing.

"Ryker told me that he would help me pick something out."

"Ryker is a good boy," Grandma states. I nod with agreement. "I'm still double checking your attire before you leave this house, though."

I don't argue.

****

What about this one?" I hear Ryker ask over Matchbox Twenty. We are in my bedroom, figuring out my attire for the party. I feel the piece of clothing he is holding up bump against my hand. The fabric is soft and it is one of my favorite shirts. I can tell because the fabric of this specific one is a lot smoother than most of them.   "What color is it?" funny how it's one of my favorite shirts and I never really cared to ask what color it was when I bought it.

"Dark purple."

I raise my eyebrows and nod, impressed.

 "Ripped jean shorts or classic?"

I pause, thinking. . . .

"Ripped," we both say at the same time. I laugh.

"Time to pick out socks!" he exclaims.

"Why do socks matter?"

"Orchid, socks *always* matter. You know the saying, 'You can always tell a girl by her socks'?"

I furrow my eyebrows. "No, where'd you hear that from?"

"My footless grandmother." I hear him shuffle through my drawers until he gets to the one with my socks and undergarments. "Well, it looks like your only options are frilly and . . . holey." he chuckles as I smack his arm.

"Alright, alright, alright," he says defensively.

"Out so I can change, Matthew McConaughey." I say, pushing him towards the door.

After I get dressed, we say goodbye to my grandparents. My curfew is eleven, but that means tenthirty in Grandparents Language. We hop into Ryker's car and he wants to stop by the supermarket to pick up soda and cups that he promised Carson he'd bring. "It'll only take a couple of minutes." he states as I hold his wrist lightly to help me follow him through the doors. The supermarket aroma always consists of baked goods and cough medicine. We weave our way throughout the aisles and Ryker finally picks out a few two-liters of different kinds of soda. He shoves two of them in my arms and we make our way towards the plastic cups, in which he also ends up placing two packs of them on my head.

I rip the packaged cups off my head as Ryker snickers and lay them on top of the sodas in my arms. We pay and leave the store, and as we get back to the car, I hear the sharp sizzle of a bottle cap opening.

"Are you drinking out of one of the two-liters?"

"Just testing it to make sure it isn't poisonous." I hear him chug and burp.

"Classy."

"Classy is as classy does." he claims as he starts the car and we drive off. When Ryker and I get to the party, anxiety begins to pulse in my chest. I hear *No Diggity* by Blackstreet pound through loudspeakers over random bursts of conversations and girls squealing with joy as they meet their friends. Ryker and I carry the soda and cups into the house and Carson and his buddies greet Ryker. Carson's house smells clean, but it's vague over the amount of cheap cologne and cigarette smoke that is wavering off of him and his posse. I act like I'm stacking cups and ignore them.

"Hey! You made it," Carson's voice stimulates over the music. It makes me cringe.

"Yeah! Pretty sick party so far, man," Ryker replies.

I still can't understand why Ryker even associates himself with Carson. Carson is the biggest screwboy in the whole school. I end up dealing with it overall but there is always still an uneasiness I have with most of his friends.

"Thanks. Hey, Orchid."

Eye-roll. "Hi." I hope no one could tell the edge on my voice if I have one, but a part of me does want them to notice it.

Ryker's hand grabs my forearm gently. It's reassuring. "We are gonna walk around and check everything out. I'll come talk in a bit." Ryker states. Carson agrees and we go our separate ways. *Thank God.*

"Can't you be nice to him for once?" Ryker says as we walk away.

"I said hi back to him."

"You had an attitude." I must not have done a good job at hiding it, then. Oh well.

"I didn't," I state. We weren't really arguing, he didn't have the arguing type of tone . . . and I don't think I do, either. But I could tell he wasn't super happy. "I just don't appreciate him being a creep. I can only imagine how many girls he has tried to get while being an indecent human being."

Ryker chuckles with agreement. "I know, he's pathetic. He's fun to play guitar with, though. That's my only argument."

Sweaty arms and legs brush against me as we make our way through the house. It is very large house, Ryker tells me. There must be a ton of people here to fill up the majority of the space that I'm feeling. As we walk, a few kids from our school say hi to Ryker and obviously not me. I'm not bothered by it, though.

As the music gets fainter, I can finally hear Ryker more clearly. "There are less people down here in the basement."

We walk carefully down the basement, and the atmosphere is calmer than upstairs. Lighter conversations are occupying the cool air as we find a small, empty couch to sit on.

"Do you want something to drink or eat?" Ryker asks.

"Drink would be great, thanks." I reply, smiling.

"Coming right up. I'll be back in a sec," he pats my leg as he gets up.

I listen to some of the conversations going on around the room as I wait, but they're boring. Some girls are talking about how far they have gotten with their boyfriends and some guys are talking about their cars. I decide to listen to the television that is on for background noise instead.   "Now on to today's top-stories," a rich, fake voice states. "A wanted man from Oathpark, Florida was spotted sometime last week coming from Georgia and is said to be occupying his hometown, incognito. . . ," *Ugh.*

So mysterious, this man. I can't help but sit numb as I listen to the report, further stating how dangerous he could be and how vague his possible whereabouts are.

The next statement made by the reporter is in a joking tone. "Apparently, he was arrested a month before passing through Oathpark for stealing a pack of cigars." a female chuckles through the television along with the reporter as my heart skips a beat.

Cigars.

"Oh my God," I whisper to myself, remembering the scent of cigar smoke coming off of the man in my backyard.

How could I be so stupid?

I need to tell Ryker.

As I start to get up, a being squished themselves next to me.

"Ryker?"

"Nope, rather better." *Carson.*

I hold back an annoyed groan. "Can I help you?"

"Why are you always so sassy with me?" he asks. I can feel his hand slightly touching my thigh. "Ryker asked the same thing earlier. My answer was: 'Because Carson is an idiot'. Please move." at least I said please.

"Hey, there's no fucking reason why you should be such a bitch to me. I'm being nice." he grips my hand when I try to stand up. I hear people begin to mutter.

"No, you're being a creep. Now let go of me," my voice is shaking with anger and fear. I move away harshly and attempt to make a run for it but his grip on me grows tighter. It instantly loosens as I hear him shout suddenly with pain.

"I can't fucking believe you Carson," Ryker yells. I feel something wet splatter my arm. "Get the fuck away from her."

I back away and smell my arm. I realize it's fruit punch and chuckle slightly at the fact that Ryker dumped our drinks on him.

"Ryker, we were just having some fun," Carson replies defensively.

"If that's your idea of fun, you need to go to a mental hospital. I trusted you and you pull this shit. You're disgusting."

"Fight!" groups of people chant around them, laughing. As loud thuds and Carson's painful groans amplify against the wall, something glass breaks, causing me to panic.

"Ryker," I shout. "Come on, he isn't worth it, it's okay, let's leave," I feel for his arm in the crowded area.

"I can't believe you, you asshole," Ryker's growl startles me and I grab his arm tightly, trying to pull. I can smell metal and something warm splatters my hand. "Ryker, you're going to kill him," I scream. I pull him as hard as I can and we both fall. I hear Carson scramble up the stairs and loud thuds pound against the stairwell as everyone follows him.

Ryker and I are both panting and I shove him away

from me, anger boiling in my heart. I get up quickly and pace myself up the stairs, ignoring Ryker's shouts and fumble to find the back door, which I eventually figure out is right next to the basement staircase and some other closed door.

I stumble out into the cool night air and take off my shoes. I follow damp stepping stones on the ground to a dirt road and walk.

As my feet pound against the rough dirt road as I walk, my frustration drains itself deep underneath my feet and toes. I can't believe all of this is happening to me at once. The one thing I've learned about being blind and living life is that I grew to not be scared of anything anymore. As I walk, fear doesn't consume me and the multiple possibilities of all the ways that I could get murdered out here don't rush around my mind. After all, the only thing we fear for darkness is what lurks deep within it.

Thunder cracks above me and the wind begins to pick up, whipping my hair away from my sweaty neck. Droplets of rain begin to hit my skin as I hear a loud muffler groan and spit behind me.

"Orchid," Ryker shouts from his car.

I ignore him and walk a little slower.

"Get in the car, Orchid. Please." Ryker's voice pleads.

I stop walking and turn slowly. "I can't believe you."
No, what I really can't believe is all of . . . this.

Everything.

The rain is beginning to pour down, its streaming droplets soaking my body and causing me to shiver despite the midsummer heat. It feels good on my pounding head.

His car door opens and slams shut. His hand grabs my arm gently and pulls. I want to protest but a sudden wave of exhaustion soaks me right along with the rain and I lean my head against him. He picks me up and carries me and sets me into the car seat next to him. He gets back into his seat and starts to drive off.

The only sound between us is the sound of rain beating against the hood of the car. It makes my headache worse.

"I was trying to protect you." Ryker says quietly, his voice hoarse from yelling.

I close my eyes and lean my wet head against the window. "I know."

"Don't be mad at me."

"I'm not, Ryker,"

"You are and I don't blame you."

"I'm truly not. I was angry a first because I was taking care of it myself just fine and I thought you went overboard. I understand that you were trying to look out for me." tears well in my eyes. I'm so tired.

An uneasy feeling wells in my stomach suddenly and I grip my chest. I turn my head with wonder as my ears start ringing. Ryker's voice chimes against my eardrums.

"I hope you know that I lo—"

The only thing that pulses in my ears during that moment are the screeching screams of the car tires and white noise clouding my every sense.

THE SOUND OF RAIN

HANA FERGUSON

<u>Chapter Nine</u>

Two girls lay in front of me. They're the same girls from my dreams.

Always the same.

We are in an open field that is on fire. The moonlight in the milky sky sticks right above the flames that blaze dark gold and rich orange, so hot that the flames almost feel cold. They lay flat on their backs, their bodies in very thin dresses, arms intertwined with each other at their sides. They aren't phased by the fire one bit. If anything, they look like they're welcoming it. The fire crackles around us and their hair is starting to singe off, but their skin is still perfect. Glossy, pale. Perfect.

Crackle.

Hiss.

The clouds of smoke graying their features.

Crackle.

Hiss.

The sound of distant screams pierce the flames with a force that moves them with their waviness.

Crackle.

Hiss.

The girls rise to their knees, their arms undone and their dresses ablaze.

Behind them, familiar footsteps crunch in the flaming grass. The rest of the figure is a black mass that is very muscular. They move in sync with the crackling and hissing of the fire like a dance. The flames kiss my naked feet and brush against my bare legs like a snake as the fire grows and rises.

Crackle.

Hiss.

They crawl to me, on their hands and knees, their burnt heads down. I stand and watch. I am numb.

Crackle.

Hiss.

They're closer, their skin still smooth and pale and glossy. Their dresses have burned off and their small breasts hang with the flames. The figure stands behind them. They are beautiful against the golden light from the fire and the moonlight that casts their crippled shadows against the charred grass that crunches beneath them.

Crackle.

Hiss.

They're under my feet, grabbing at my ankles, scratching my legs to bits of muscle that melt against

their palms. They look straight up at me. Their eyes are violet.

They know.

They know me.

They plead for me to know them, but I can't.

I want to, because they are so familiar. I can't.

I want these dreams to end.

They continue to grab me and pull at my skin that is nonexistent as I scream with the flames that lick all three of us into a freezing cold sensation that numbs every nerve I have.

Crackle.

Hiss.

I scream with agony and frustration and sadness. I scream for them.

Crackle.

Hiss.

I scream. . . ,

. . .because they have me.

<u>Chapter Ten</u>

The only time I've ever seen a form—the smallest form ever *and* a form that was outside of my dreams—was when I was with one of my many eye doctors. I was nine and Grandpa and I were at the ophthalmologist. I was getting my eyes checked for the millionth time, two years after the accident. For at least three years after it occurred, I'd get my eyes checked every month.

My ophthalmologist's name was Dr. Sarah Missioner. She was very nice; and because she was nice, I assumed she was also probably pretty. Her voice sounded young and energetic. She gave me a handful of Jolly Ranchers after every check up.

The small form I saw was just a ball of light. It was so small I almost didn't see it. She was testing my eyes— she must have been doing some sort of light exercise with my eyes or looking into them with multiple different lights—and a little white orb formed behind my numb, black eyeballs. I gasped and I heard Dr. Missioner's chair jolt. Her hand and light moved with her.

"No, no! Keep it there," I scrunched my eyebrows and focus on where I thought I saw the orb.

"She sees something," Grandpa claimed, astonished. I focused and focused and focused. My head was pounding.

After what seemed like an hour, I saw the orb. It was small and white. It had a shape to it that made it glow even more.

"Can you see something, Orca?"

"Yes," I replied numbly, still looking at the orb. It floated slightly to the left. I followed it with my eyes.

Dr. Missioner didn't say anything. I felt her eyes on me.

"Dr. Missioner, stop the light for a moment,"

"I turned the light off twenty minutes ago."

My heart skipped a beat. "What?"

"You're seeing something else."

"How's that possible?" Grandpa asked.

"I have no idea," Dr. Missioner breathed.

We sat there for probably another hour. The orb still held its place, floating white with gray speckles.

"It has a shape to it, Dr. Missioner," I whispered.

"What is the shape?"

"I can't tell . . . I'm trying really hard to focus."

"Don't strain yourself honey, if you can't see it, don't jeopardize your eyes even more,"

"I'm not, I'm trying to figure out if it's real or something that is just making itself up in my head," I replied. "I think it might be getting bigger."

"Getting bigger? Is something growing behind her eyes?" Grandpa asked.

"I've never seen anything like this," Dr. Missioner said. "She might be developing Charles Bonnet Syndrome."

"Syndrome?" I asked. Anything with the word 'syndrome' doesn't sound good at all.   "Yes. You're seeing random shapes and hallucinations," she said. "Is this recent or has this been happening?"

"The shape is just now happening. I've been having dreams that I can see in."

"Charles Bonnet Syndrome sounds pretty accurate to me," she confirmed. "You see in your dreams?"

"I see in my dreams."

"What do you see?"

The white shape grew larger when she asked this—
it exploded in front of my eyes like a white firework. I
screamed and cradled my head in my hands. There was
no pain; just white light.

"It's gone now," I groaned. "It's gone."

"Did you catch the shape, Orchid?" Dr. Missioner
asked.

"An explosion I've seen before," I replied. "I've
seen this explosion—the shape—before."

"Tell me more about your dreams," Dr. Missioner
said. She wrapped her arms around me when I began
sobbing. "Tell me what is in your dreams Orchid, I'm
here to help you."

"I want to know where the explosion came from," I
cried. "Grandpa, where was the explosion?"

Grandpa was silent for a second before he
answered.
"The one behind your eyes, Orchid? The doctor said you
might have Charles Bonnet Syndrome,"

"No, something bad happened, something very bad
happened, I can feel it Grandpa, make it stop!" I cried
harder. Dr. Missioner calmed me down. Heels clacked
against the floor of the room and Dr. Missioner pulled

me up in the chair and wiped my eyes.

"Is everything okay in here?" the heels stopped and asked.

"Yes Aria, she is just a little upset right now," Aria was the office secretary. "It's okay, Orchid."

"Can I get you some water?" Aria's voice asked.
I sniffled and shook my head.

"I think we'd better come back tomorrow," Grandpa said.

"Okay. I'll schedule an appointment for tomorrow. Both of you have a good rest of your day."

Dr. Missioner and I went through our same ritual—she gave me a hug and a handful of Jolly Ranchers. The handful of candies this time felt a lot bigger. Dr. Missioner was doing that to make me feel better, but I felt the same. The white firework that formed behind my eyes made me shake. With my cheeks still wet, I sucked on a blue raspberry Jolly Rancher as we walked out of the doors.

The phenomenon behind my eyes was never spoken of again. Grandma doesn't know. I knew something, but I ignored it. I felt something, but I ignored it. I ignored the painstaking curiosity that manifested my thoughts.

Dangerously, I ignored all of the years to come; and they're here.

HANA FERGUSON

Chapter Eleven

I gasp awake.

My dreams are back! I exclaim in my head. I re-think everything and realize, *how was I asleep? I don't remember falling asleep.*

The last thing I remember was . . . oh, God.

The party.

Realizing the odd familiarity of the missing man that was in my backyard.

Carson.

Ryker.

Walking in the rain and getting into Ryker's car.

The uneasy feeling and the screech of the tires and the sharp pain against my head that was leaning, turned, against the window.

Oh, God. Ryker.

I'm awake, but my I can feel my eyes are still closed. I move my hands and feel cords and silky fabric hooked all around me. The rooms smells like medicine and rubbing alcohol. My face is extremely sore and puffy and I feel raw on the inside of my stomach and throat. I see the gloaming blackness I always see, but it's different. It's not as dark.

In fact, could that be a light above me?

I pry my eyes open very slowly and a white light shocks the sockets that hold them and they begin to throb.

What the hell is going on?

I throw my palms up to my sore eyes and rub them for a moment before putting them back down at my aching sides. I try to open my eyes again. I turn my head away to the side and downwards this time. My neck is in a lot of pain.

I open my eyes slower than I did before. Light shocks them again for a split moment, but they focus on what is in front of me.

I see two feet crossed at the ankles, wearing blue jeans and black Converse. They're scuffed up a bit and dirty. They're situated calmly on the clean tiled floor.

Am I dreaming right now? Why am I able to see?

My eyes wander upwards, causing me to squint, and the individual is wearing a black Nirvana shirt. My eyes wander farther up and slower as my heart pounds against my bruised chest. The individual is male and he is asleep.

Oh my God.

Oh my God.

Oh. My. God.

His face looks just as I'd felt. Sharp jawline, parted and longish brown hair. Beautiful lips that have dried blood on them. A dried, bloody nose. The same exact scar.

Ryker. He is so *handsome.*

I sit up slowly, looking around the room. It's just the two of us.

Where are Grandma and Grandpa?

I look out the hospital privacy window and I see an occasional bystander or nurse walk by. I look back at Ryker. Still asleep.

I swing my legs over the bed, rub my tender eyes again gently. My finger gets caught in a tube hooked in my nose and I untangle it. I push myself up. I force away a painful groan from escaping my body as I stand up and make my way towards his chair. I kneel on the ground beside his chair and lean my arms and chin on the wooden armrest, studying his face. I reach up to his nose where there is dried blood and rub gently underneath it with my thumb. The feeling of blood is familiar but it feels different now that I can actually see it. I can feel his face start to twitch awake, but I don't move my thumb.

The cords are stretching from me moving so I pull them gently to make them more lenient to the monitors. I look out the open hospital window and the sky streaks with pink and orange. I look at the clock but I can't tell time on that one so I glance at a digital one on the nightstand next to me. It's eight o'clock in the evening.

I do a double-take, though, of what is next to the clock on the wall above my bed.

There is a small, circular woven piece of cloth with feathers hanging down it pinned to the wall, right above my wrinkled pillow. It is dark purple and it has intricate string work in the middle of the circle. I stare at it for a few moments in hopes of figuring out what it is—and I realize it is a dream catcher.

I smile lightly, assuming Ryker brought it, and listen to the beeps of the machines. I hear a patient arguing with a nurse as I watch the sky change into a bruised purple before I hear a deep breath and a sleepy sigh above me. Ryker's eyes open, looking right at me. From the side, the light lightens them and they're crystal blue.

THE SOUND OF RAIN

"Orchid?"

I rub my eyes that are watering—not from crying,
but from the light I'm not used to that is irritating them—
and look up, straight into his eyes.

"Yes?"

He furrows his eyebrows and moves his head to the
side. My eyes follow him.

He moves his hand in front of me. My eyes follow
once again.

"Oh my God. . . ," he whispers. He bends down and
crushes me in a hug. I hold my breath and bear the pain
because I love the feeling of his arms around me, even if
it feels like my insides are about to explode. I know for a
fact that my heart will, right in this moment.

He wipes my eyes for me gently. He stands up and
helps me sit on the bed and hands me a bottle of Coke
from the table. I chug it and the carbonation burns my
throat but I'm so thirsty I can't put it down until every
last bit of it is gone. I toss the bottle into the garbage
can. The quick movement startles me.

We sit in silence for a moment. His eyes don't leave

me.

I turn back to him. "What happened?"

He rubs his nose. There is still a little bit of blood underneath.

"Well, we went to Carson's party, and he start—"

"I remember what happened at the party. I meant what happened in the car." what a miracle that I remember. Why can't I remember what happened after the first accident?

"Right. The rain started pouring even harder after I finally got your stubborn ass into the car," *the sound of rain pounding against the hood of the car.* "I could see, but we were on dirt back-roads coming from Carson's and the speed limit is a lot faster and out of nowhere, other headlights collided with mine on your side of the car and you were unconscious because your head busted the window completely and I was awake and I called the ambulance and the other car fled," Ryker rambles on, his facial expression strained. It's weird seeing people's face change as they talk. I wrap my arms around him and lean my head into his chest. His heartbeat is still the same.

"I'm so sorry," he mumbles into my hair.

"Don't be sorry. I can see now," I mumble back.

"Now you can see the issues of the world *and* feel them."

"That's called being a normal human being with normal senses."

"You're still physically hurt."

"Doesn't hurt that bad."

"Your heart hurts."

I hesitate, because he's right. Instead, I mumble back a mouth-full of lies. "Doesn't hurt that bad."

Ryker replies with a sigh deep in his chest that raises my face. He pats my back and lets go of me.

"Are you hurt?" I ask, sitting back.

"No. Just a few cuts and bruises. You took most of the damage."

"Besides the car,"

He rubs his face hard with his palms. "Don't remind me."

"I'm sorry."

"Don't ever be sorry for this," he says. "I better call

the nurse in here and tell her you're awake."

I nod, rubbing my damp eyes. "Thank you for the dream catcher," I state lightly.

He smiles. "You're welcome, Orchid. I ran into Carson a while ago. He told me he is sorry. He told me to tell you he is really sorry and that he feels bad."

I feel a pang of guilt. "He is a stupid teenage boy. Apology accepted. Where is Grandma and Grandpa?"

"They were here for the last two days that you've been here. So have I, but I told them I'd stay longer so that they could go home and get some rest and pack a bag for you."

"Two days?" I ask, astonished. He smiles tightly and nods.

"If you want to leave, you can," I say.

"Trying to get rid of me already? You've only seen me for ten minutes. Is it because you think I look ugly?" I laugh, but stop because it jolts my ribs painfully.

"You're far from ugly. Go get the nurse and leave for a while. I'll be fine. Go sleep in a real bed."

"Are you—"

"Yes, I'm sure. Get out." I smile.

He laughs lightly and kisses the top of my head, walking to the door. "I'll be back."

"'Kay, *Terminator*."

He looks back at me, leaning against the doorway. The biggest smile spreads across his face.

That smile is something, out of almost everything else I have forgotten, that I can't forget.

The nurse comes in after a while and checks basically every aspect of my body and sticks different IV's up my arms. She takes out my feeding tube. Needles hurt more now that I can see them being poked in my skin. She hands me a sheet of paper with the hospital's cafeteria menu on it and a pen. I didn't realize how hungry I was since I woke up. I look through the list, making out the written English in my head slowly, and hold the pen in my hand. The feeling of watching myself write is completely foreign. There are small pictures of the food next to each item. I carefully swipe crooked marks with the pen next to two cheese personal-pan pizzas, a banana for later, and four bottles of water. The Coke I drank earlier makes my stomach gurgle uncomfortably.

I hand her the sheet and pen and read her name-tag. "What's your name?"

She smiles. Her skin is leather-tan and her hair is so black it almost looks purple under the hospital lights. Her eyes are large and dark. She is young and very pretty. "Maria. I'm from Brazil," she says. Her accent rolls against my ears.

"Must be beautiful there."

"There is plenty to see," she replies. "I heard you were blind."

"Ryker told you?" I ask. Well, duh, he told her. She's my nurse.

"Your friend, yes. Not sure how that happened?" I sit in silence for a moment, evaluating her accent and wondering if she's asking herself or me. I shake my head no.

"Neither do I. A lot of things happen for a reason, no?" I shrug.

"I've talked to the doctor and he was very surprised

THE SOUND OF RAIN

as well. He will come in to check on you after you eat."
"Have you ever seen a situation like mine?" I ask. She
scrunches her face with thought.

"Nothing like it. But everything will be okay," Maria
says. She is very sweet and convincing.

Everything will be okay.

She takes a small flashlight out of her scrubs pants
pocket and clicks it on. "This might be very bright but
I'm going to check your eyes."

She shines the light in my eyes and I gasp with
shock. My eyes might as well be called Orchid Falls at
the rate that they're watering. I close and rub them, but
force myself to look up.

"They're a little yellow and splotched with red,"
Maria claims. "The pupils seem fine besides extreme
dilation." sounds *super* healthy to me. "I'm going to give
them eye drops."

After she pours basically a whole bottle of eye drops
into my eyes, she tells me that she will be back with my
food soon. I tell her thank you and lean back into the
pillows and rub my eyes. I want to know every single
thing about the accident. Not the one I just had. The one

that killed my mom. The one that caused my father to flee. The one that triggered the nightmares (I wouldn't consider them dreams anymore). The one that changed my life forever, into a walking, blind, psychological mishap.

****

I eat and sit in the hospital room alone. I figure that Grandma, Grandpa, and Ryker won't come to visit me until tomorrow. I don't mind that, though. I want to be alone to gather my thoughts and regain my sanity. I already know that I probably won't sleep tonight. Partially because my nerves are sliced in a half like electrical cords and sparking with adrenaline and because I'm afraid of what my dreams (nightmares!) will have in store. I'm not ready for that kind of psychological damage quite yet.

The doctor comes in around ten at night and figure he is working the night shift. I'm thankful.

He isn't super old—maybe in his early fifties—and his gray hair swoops like tinsel on the right side of his face. He wears typical doctor attire and a stethoscope around his neck.

"Orchid, you're awake," he says, smiling.
"I'm Dr. Philip Gregor."
"I sure am. Nice to meet you."

"I already know you," he says. My stomach jumps. "I took care of you the first round."

Oh. He means from when I was a kid; the first accident.

"Unfortunate that we are meeting again through this way. How are you feeling?"

"Weird."

"That's normal," Dr. Gregor says. "Maria did a good job taking care of you. Your friend really cares about you, huh?"

"He's a very good friend," I reply, rubbing my eyes.

"Indeed. Don't rub, it'll make them worse," he says as he pats my wrist away from my face gently. "He's been staying here with you all day and night." His thin lips and dimpled chin crease into a smile. "I've been giving anti-inflammatories, pain killers, and I did give you a muscle relaxer while you were asleep. The IV's were mainly used for feeding your body while you were asleep during that full forty-eight hour period. After your stay here, I'll prescribe typical painkillers or ones that are a little stronger, depending on your pain level when you leave. You might experience migraines and dizzy spells for the next couple of weeks. The pain in your neck is from whiplash. It's really a miracle that you didn't split your head wide open."

"That's real comforting to hear." I say bluntly. He laughs.

"I like you. You're very practical and laugh at the situation."

"I guess. It's kind of hard to laugh right now, though. My ribs feel like they're caving in."

"Bruised deeply. That'll heal. I'm not going to give you sleeping medication right now though since I figured that you'd want to be awake for a little while. Plus I can't mix that many medications at once." he sits on the bed next to me and flips a notebook out. I peek over it.

"This is your hospital registration sheet and prescriptions," he says as he scans through it. "Just making sure everything I told you by memory was correct. So, you were blind before this—quite a miracle?"

"Do you believe it?"

"Never said I didn't. I'm assuming you don't though."

"It's nearly impossible to believe," I say. "I'm not sure what to believe anymore. Everything is wrong. Everything has been wrong."

He closes his notebook and lays it beside him on the bed.

"You shouldn't live to try to explain everything to everyone," he says. His response shocks me, to be honest. It's actually sapient. "I have a minor in psychology and I can read a person's story just by looking at them. That's why it's helpful to be a doctor, as well. Figuring someone out makes it easier to help them.

I want you to know that if someone doesn't believe you, even when you're telling the truth, walk away."

"Should I walk away from you?"

Dr. Gregor laughs. "No. I believe you. I believe what I discovered ten years ago. I believe your friend Ryker is a very believable character."

"Very interesting character indeed. I've known him basically my whole life. I think we might be more than friends now. But sometimes he doesn't always understand things when it comes to me and my problems." this dude really knows how to make a person open up naturally even when they're not used to opening up, like, at all.

What a freakin' pro.

"Either he doesn't understand, or he doesn't *want* to understand." Dr. Gregor states.

"You think he chooses to shut me out?"

"Emotionally? Probably. It has to go very deep for him to do that, though. Your bond is too close for him to shut you out that much. There must have been something that happened in the past with you two that triggers him."

"Can you tell me what happened? During the first accident," I ask.

"I can't tell you what I don't truly know, Orchid." I look down at my hands in my crossed lap with amazement. I need to talk to Ryker as soon as possible.

"I think once you feel better, you two should talk it

out. Till then, please don't stress about it. I know it's dumb for me to ask that, but you really need to focus on healing. We are planning three more days for your visit at least so that I can monitor your health and eyes." he gets up with a grunt and grabs his notebook.
"Thank you for the advice. I need a lot of it right now."

"You're very welcome. You're a very smart girl. Everything works out in the end."

"I'm not looking for a happy ending," I state. He leans on the door frame, his back to me. "Just a somewhat decent one is all I want, truly."

"Happy endings don't always exist. Decent ones do more than completely happy ones. But the only thing that is for-sure with endings is that there is always an ending for something regardless. Some experience very unfortunate ones. Most of us are lucky enough to experience the decent ones."

Dr. Phillips walks out of the door and closes it. I lean back on the bed and sigh, not believing this is happening to me. I'm not sure what to think of anything at this point, to be completely honest. I guess besides the fact that I can magically see all of a sudden, my real intention right now is to figure out what happened so long ago that has burned so many bridges.

After all of the pizza and water that I've consumed, I need to use the restroom. I carefully get up without acting like I'm going to break every bone in my body and make my way to the bathroom door. I shove it open and flicker the light on, rubbing my eyes again. I do my business and move towards the sink to wash my hands and look up in the mirror. I turn the faucet off and step back, studying myself with amazement. My hair is fairly close enough to as I'd described it before. It's a bit messy from my pillow and greasy from the lack of washing it. My face isn't nearly as I'd described it, mainly because of the puffiness and bruises, but that'll go away. I don't look too bad, I think.

I decide to take a quick shower, fix my bed, and attempt to get some rest. I hope that tomorrow brings a new life. I need it.

THE SOUND OF RAIN

<u>Chapter Twelve</u>

I'm sitting up in the hospital bed, watching the sunrise. I've woken up at least six times in the last five hours due to head pain and fluctuations of terrifying scenarios fuzzing in and out of my head. I finally decided to stay awake after the fourth time once I knew that I couldn't fall back asleep. My face is puffy and irritated and my neck is sore but not as sore as it was before. Maria is just starting her shift and she comes in to check on me. She smells like coffee and hairspray. She hands me some Ibuprofen that I doubt will work, but I take it anyway. I order breakfast while she's in here with me: two bagels with plain cream cheese and a large iced coffee. She smiles and tells me that she will bring it in about half an hour since the kitchen is just now starting to prepare fresh food.

I decide to get up and walk around my room a little bit. I see that there is a chunky brown phone across the bed on a table. I'm tempted to call Grandma and Grandpa but I know that they're still sleeping. I ignore it and go into the bathroom and prop the door open. As I begin to freshen up, I hope that Ryker will come soon with some normal clothes. I'm in the same hospital gown and shorts that I've been wearing and I really want to change. I comb my hair and carefully wash my face gently and apply antibiotic cream on my facial wounds. Maria comes in with my breakfast and she looks around, spotting me in the bathroom.

"Wait there just a second, I will be right back." Maria says as she sets the food down on the table by the phone and quickly jogs out of the room. I comb my hair lightly some more as I wait; and she stumbles in with a bottle of . . . something.

"Here. This is hair oil," she says as she pumps some into my hand. It is warm and it smells fruity. "Rub it in your hair like this."

Maria ruffles her almost-purple hair around with her fingers and I do the same with mine. It instantly feels softer as the oil hydrates my short peachy curls, making them bouncier.

Maria feels my hair and smiles. "Very nice?"

I nod and smile. "Thank you."

"You keep. I have an extra bottle."

Maria smiles and grabs a smaller bottle out of her breast scrubs pocket: eye drops. I lean my head hack as she squirts them into my eyeballs, causing them to burn slightly. I shut my eyes for a couple of minutes to let them soak in like she tells me and she applies cool medicated eye patches underneath my eyes.

"They are medicated so they will help your eyes heal a bit quicker. They also help with puffiness and it will help the skin around your eyes become pretty again." Maria explains. I tell her thank you and she turns to leave.

I smell the hair oil bottle again and smile, set it down on the table, and grab my breakfast. I make my way over to the big chair I pushed near the window before and pull it towards the end of my bed where I can see the television better. I sit down and click the television on and the first channel that pops up is the local news channel so I continue to watch it to catch up on what I've missed. I grab the plastic butter knife and fork that is taped to a small container of cream cheese and rip it off. As I spread cream cheese on both of my warm, toasty bagels, I listen to the news. The anchorman's voice is familiar.

"Friday night, a hit-and-run occurred off the back roads Plymouth and Williker right here in Oathpark, causing the passenger to be transferred into hospitalization and the driver was stable enough to call

for help. The opposite vehicle was occupied by a man who seemed to be in his late forties, as the driver claims as he saw through one of his dimmed headlights, and that he drove off before he could get any more legal information that could have helped with this case."
I groan. This news anchor needs a new day job. When can I *not* get a reminder?

I chomp into my bagel and take a sip of my iced coffee. It instantly wakes me up and I feel a lot better, despite the news I just received. I force myself to listen to more of the news until it changes to the local weather.

I finish my food and sigh, looking at my empty tray. The crumbs sitting on the plate are in the shape of a lopsided heart, ironically enough. Hearts are the last thing I come to think of right now. Maria comes and takes my tray and hands me two painkillers. I take them from her but the pain isn't as bad today so I just set the pills on my side-table. I turn the television off and pull the chair back over to the window. I sit and look out the window and watch the cars whipping by below me, their colors glaring with the sun. I check the clock and it's noon.

After a while, I hear work boots stomping against the floor and plastic bags ruffling. I turn around and

Ryker is holding four grocery bags full of clothes, hygiene products, and a couple books, and my radio. I stand up quickly and smile the biggest smile I've smiled in a while.

Ryker sets the stuff down on the bed and smiles.

"Looks like you're healing up pretty good," I nod.

"Feeling a little better?"

I nod again. "I think once I take a genuine shower and put on fresh clothes I'll be a new person. Are Grandma and Grandpa here?"

"They said they'll be over soon. The bathroom piping busted at your house and my uncle is helping them fix it."

"If it's not one thing it's another," I reply.

Ryker chuckles and gives me a side-hug. "Don't worry. There is nothing that can't be fixed. Go shower."

I hug him back. "Thank you, I truly appreciate it." I take the bag of clothes with me into the bathroom and shut the door. It felt good to shower the other night but it sucked putting the same clothes on.

I turn the hot water on and shower, using actual shampoo and soap that Ryker brought me. After I finish, I pick out one of the T-shirts in the bag and unfold it. It's a shirt with The Cranberries' logo on it. I feel the vinyl print on the front and recognize the smooth texture. I put it on along with my undergarments and a pair of sweatpants. I also throw on a pair of hospital socks that lay neatly folded on the sink because I need as much comfort as I can get. I comb my hair and rub some more of the oil Maria gave me into my damp locks. I put on deodorant (I've never missed deodorant so much in my life) and brush my teeth. I feel amazing. I can't wait until my face heals up so I'll look amazing eventually, too. I'll just have to deal with how I feel for now.

"The Cranberries!" Ryker exclaims with an air guitar move as I walk out. I roll my eyes and laugh. "Wanna go on a little walk?"

"I can't leave the hospital campus," I state.

"We can walk *around* the campus Dumbo," he says.

"Did I gain weight too while I've been here?"

"No, why would you ask that?" he asks as we walk out the door. I tell one of the nurses that we are just walking around and she has us sign our names on a sheet of paper.

"You just referred to me as a baby elephant,"

"Oh, yeah, I guess that's true. I didn't realize his name in the movie was actually Dumbo."

"It's the title of the movie," I state, widening my eyes.

Ryker goes silent and rolls his eyes. His answer whenever he knows he's wrong.

"And you call me Dumbo."

"Hey, that elephant got his feelings hurt really bad. I think I want to be his friend more than your's right now. Isn't it a Disney movie?"

"He is a cute elephant. Elephants are my favorite animal and I love Disney. I can't believe how uncultured you are." I reply as we link our arms together, pushing open the glass doors. The sun is very bright and I turn away quickly, putting my hands over my eyes.

"Shit, I forgot. You haven't been outside yet, have you?" I answer with a shake of my head and a groan.

"One second, stay right here. Keep your eyes covered."

THE SOUND OF RAIN

I hear him quickly run back into the hospital. A minute or so later I hear him come back and he puts his hand on my arm. This feeling is familiar; not seeing and still feeling his touch. The connection isn't as strong.

"Put these on,"

I reach my hand out and take the hard, smooth object. They're sunglasses. I put them on.

I open my eyes and look over at him. I can see him clearly; he's just a bit darker than normal. I look all around me. The trees, the grass, the decorative flowers the hospital has planted everywhere. I take off the sunglasses partially and look around slowly. I'm looking into the mirror of my dreams; the reality of the greens and blues and purples shocking my eyes like they're pieces of candy that my eyes eat up immediately.

"I've missed you." Ryker hugs my side.

"I've missed you, too." I hug him back. "Have you been playing guitar? I miss your guitar."

He scoffs. "Not as much as I probably should, no. We will do more lessons once you get better."

"The competition is coming up soon," I say.

"I know. I'll make sure I wow you."

"Shouldn't be that hard." Ryker squints in the sun and smiles.

"Have you talked to the doctor recently?"

I nod.

"Did he tell you anything?"

I nod again. "Some things, mainly what's wrong with me right now," we walk down the path farther and towards the back of the building. I look at him. Still cute as ever. "I still can't believe I can see all of a sudden. No one understands it and I don't know if it should be a miracle or a horrifying reality because I don't know how it happened or if it was supposed to happen."

"Obviously it's a miracle, Orchid. It's a weird situation but you're over-reacting,"

"I don't think I am. I'm just questioning it,"

"Questioning God yet?"

"His tactics."

"Fair enough," he replies. "Speaking of Gods . . . want to see The Rolling Stones with me on Tuesday?"

"You're crazy." I scoff. He's casually babbling.

"Exactly right when you're able to leave this hospital. If you think I'm joking, I'm not."

I stop and look over at him. He doesn't look like he's joking at all.

"We really are going to see The Rolling Stones?"

"I really want to. We need to get out of here for a while. Their date closest to Oathpark is only an hour away."

We continue walking and I hug his side again as we walk. "I can't leave for another two days."

"I know."

"Doctor is very nice."

"I know. Very wise. When I was a mess, blaming myself for the accident, he gave me a handful of words . . . and all of them contained wisdom. So much wisdom."

"Same here, surprisingly."

"You need it."

"Wisdom?"

"No, words. Someone to talk to."

"I have you."

"Shouldn't always be me."

"There isn't anything wrong with having one person."

"There is when that one person is broken themselves,"

"Broken people are the best people."

"Broken people cause problems."

"Are you saying I cause problems?"

"If anything, you're fixed. But no. I do."

"How do you cause problems, Ryker?"

"You don't know the half of it,"

"Have you done something? Why are you acting like this?"

"The accident, Orchid,"

"That wasn't your fault, you idiot," I say this seriously. He is being an idiot.

"All of this feels like it's my fault,"

"But it isn't," I reply as he pulls away from me and stuffs his hands in his pockets. His face and skin look dead in the dark shade of the sunglasses.

We go over to a bench and sit. He sits and rubs his face. He's silent for a moment and then looks up. His eyes are watery. "It feels like my fault."

"It isn't your fault at all," I say, pulling him to me. I can feel his tears against my shirt. "Do you hear me? None of this is,"

Ryker makes a muffled sobbing sound. I've never seen him like this before and it makes me want to recoil. I hold onto him.

We sit like this for a while until he calms down. I pull his face up and kiss his damp cheeks.

"Everything is okay. I'm okay, you're okay. Grandma and Grandpa will be here soon, and guess what? They're okay, too." I say. He kisses the corner of my mouth and wipes his nose. I rub his back and I remember the guy on the news.

"I think the dude that's been coming around here and the one that was in my backyard is the dude who hit us, Ryker."

He doesn't say anything. He wipes his eyes and sets

his chin on his hands that are propped up by his elbows on his knees.

"It makes sense," I say again.

He eventually breaks the silence. He has a weird look on his face. He's hurt. He's angry. But most of all, he knows something. I know he does, but I ignore the feeling.

"Yeah, it does. And we're going to get him."

"Yes, we are," he squeezes my shoulders and sighs as he stands. "Let's go back in and wait for Grandma and Grandpa. I'll pick us up some lunch. You pick anywhere you want."

We head back in and see Maria at the front desk talking to the other nurse we saw walking out. We ask her if she knows if Grandma and Grandpa are here yet and she says she doesn't know.

We get back to the room and I sit on the bed.

"What do you want for lunch?" Ryker asks.

"Anything is fine,"

"So you want pickled liver and horseradish for lunch?"

THE SOUND OF RAIN

"Ew. You know what I mean."

"Pickled beets?"

An instant flashback occurs. The vinegar bath and remembering Grandpa's pickled beets.

"Those don't sound bad at all. Only if they were Grandpa's."

"I was just joking, but I did say I'd get you anything you want."

"He still has leftover beets behind one of the cupboards but they're probably well over six years old."

"Still a cute decoration. They're your's. What do you want for real food, though?"

"Surprise me,"

"Alrighty."

Ryker leaves the room and I click the television on. I want to see Grandma and Grandpa really bad. I really miss them, especially Grandpa. I wonder if they've watched the news.

I flick through the channels and see that Forensic Files is on. It's hard for me to read the description so I just close out of it. I think the hardest part about seeing again is that I have to re-learn how to read and write. I skim past the words but it's still difficult to make out something that looks like alphabet soup. I put my sunglasses back on (Maria told me as she just came in that I can only have one hour of television a day and I have to wear sunglasses when I watch it). The narrator's voice gives me chills.

I lay down for a while and watch. This one is about an accidental drowning case switched to murder. I get up and close the blinds because the sun that is blaring through them are bothering me, and I see two old people in the parking lot walking. They look like ants walking up to the doors. I can't make out their faces but the tops of their heads shimmer gray in the sunlight.

I quickly go back to the bed and cover up and switch the television off. I take my sunglasses off and act like I'm somewhat trying to sleep.

Do Grandma and Grandpa know that I can see? I never thought of asking Ryker that and he never told me whether or not that he told them. I'm not sure if that's truly them but my heart begins to beat so hard in my chest I think it's going to burst into flames. The thumps burn up my throat.

THE SOUND OF RAIN

As I lay there, I try to control my breathing. I cover up with the covers more, but not too much so that my eyes aren't covered. I don't ever want them to be covered again.

A door handle turns and I squeeze my eyes shut momentarily before opening them again with the click of the door closing. A familiar shuffle scuffles across the hospital tiles. I open my eyes slowly and sit up.

"Orchid," he says, his voice distraught.

"Grandpa," I reply. A smile spreads across his face. He is so familiar—old yet still the same as I remember him. His mustache is gray. He looks around at me like he doesn't know I can see. I look right into his eyes and they glisten.

"My little Orca," he says as he shuffles over to me. He sits on the bed slowly and wraps his arms around me. "You're very handsome, Grandpa," I say. Tears burn my eyes.

"My Orca can see!" Grandpa exclaims as he squeezes me tighter. He smells like coffee. I rub my face into his shirt taking in his familiar scent and laugh.

"Yes, I can see the whole world now,"

"Not only can you still feel it, you can see it now,"
"Yes, Grandpa, you're exactly right." basically the same conversation I had with Ryker. So far so good.

"I love you my sweet granddaughter,"

"I love you, Grandpa."

We hug a little while longer and I look over at Grandma. She is standing in the doorway and her cheeks are glittery under the hospital lights.

"Come here, Grandma." I say.

She walks over to me. Her hair is a light reddish-brown with gray silver streaks and it sways against her shoulders as she walks. I don't think her face has aged at all; barely a wrinkle captures it.

sits on the other side of me and all three of us squeeze each other.

"It's a miracle," Grandma says.

"I know. The doctors are trying to figure out how it happened."

"It must be God's work," she replies.

"I don't know."

"It has to be,"

"I don't know." I say again. I'm not sure what to trust or believe in right now but I don't crush Grandma's assertion.

We all pull away from each other.

"Did you fix the plumbing, Grandpa?"

"I did, indeed," his mustache moves as he speaks. "Also have a lot of work to do still at the shop with that new addition."

"I understand. You're a hard worker."

Grandpa pats my back.

"I talked you your doctor, dear," Grandma interrupts.

"You know you need to stay in for another day or two right? They haven't done too many tests quite yet but they're going to send in a couple of professionals to investigate probably sometime later today or tomorrow."

"I know," I say. "Do you have any information on who hit Ryker's car? I've been seeing it all over the news." "I don't, besides what's being stated on the media, honey."

"You sure?" I ask. I'm beginning to push it. I don't expect Grandpa to say anything and I don't blame him and his fragile self. I blame Grandma, though. She never tells me anything and I'm sick of her playing mind games.

"You know something and you need to tell me."

"Orchid, whatever you're talking about, there is nothing. There is nothing left to say. I don't know, Orchid."

Her hands begin to tremble. She's trying not to break.

"Let's just enjoy each other's company," Grandpa states. "None of us need this kind of stress right now." Grandma sits down in the chair next to my bed and I stare at her as she moves.

I ignore Grandpa's wishes. "Grandma, I need to know."

"You were in a car accident. That's all there is to it,"

"No, ten years ago," I state. "You know and you won't tell me. I'm not ten anymore. I'm almost an adult, basically an adult now, and I deserve to know." Grandpa watches us with worry but doesn't say anything. I put a hand on his arm comfortingly and look up at him. His face tells me I'm doing the right thing but he is still uneasy. I turn to Grandma, who still isn't saying anything.

"I just wanted to protect you," she finally says after a few long, painful moments of intriguing silence. "I've been hiding you from the real world because all I've wanted to do is to protect you from anymore harm." her voice cracks and she puts her head in her hands. Her face is contorted, a mixture of sorrow and fear. It's foreign and my heart breaks as she sobs. I need to be firm with her, though.

"What happened, Grandma?" I ask. I wait for her to gather herself. Grandpa goes over to her and rubs her back. She sniffles, wipes her face, and looks up at me.

"A lot. A lot happened," she says. "Your father, your mother . . . Ryker. Everyone has been affected." she was going to say an additional name besides my father, mother, and Ryker.

"Who else?" I ask.

"I just said everybody has been affected. Was affected." "There is someone else that you were going to mention besides my father and mother and Ryker."

"Everyone."

I realize that she isn't going to excel any further and tell me who else so I continue. "What happened?"

"Your father was an alcoholic," Grandma states. "A very bad one. He couldn't go an hour without at least a sip of liquor." she looks around the room, a fearful look in her eyes. Grandpa goes up to the door and shuts it.

I adjust myself on the hospital bed, listening to her, watching her with intent.

"Your mother didn't love him anymore and wanted to leave him. To take you with her and leave for good. I told her to come to us and stay." Grandma pulls a cigarette out of her purse with a shaky hand. She grabs her lighter and attempts to light it, but her fingers slip. I grab the lighter and light it for her. She sucks in and puffs a ball of smoke out of her thin, wrinkled lips slowly.

"Your father was an asshole. That's all there is to it. He hurt your mother very badly."

"What else?"

"That is it." she takes a long drag of her cigarette. She is back to her unwilful old self. I roll my eyes.

"Bullshit."

"Watch your mouth."

"Tell me,"

"That is all you need to know for now."

"I want to know every single thing." my blood boils. Right when I think she's going to tell me, finally tell me everything I've been wanting to know for the last ten years, she drops. She is absolutely unbearable. I can't be around her anymore without wanting to pull every single frizzy strand of my hair.

She sits up and puts her cigarette out in the chipped glass ashtray the hospital left out. I watch her move slowly. I forgot that Grandpa is sitting next to me; he is so quiet.

"I can't believe you," I snap. "I don't want to be around you anymore. I refuse to."

"Orchid Jane, you will. I am your guardian."

"No, Grandpa is. You're not. You don't deserve the title—you won't even fess up what happened."

"I gave you all of the information you needed. There is a difference between needs and wants." She is furious now. I don't care anymore. I hope I break her as much as she has broken me.

"I will never blame Grandpa for hiding from you," I

say. "I will never blame him for not telling me anything because that isn't his job. It's your's. You claim to know everything but you know not a word. And what you do know you won't even tell me. I blame you. I blame your cowardice. I don't want to see you until something changes."

She is quiet. I stare at her—my eyes burning into her hot face. Beads of sweat glisten above her eyebrow. I accept her decision after a few long moments. I think everything over in my head quickly and I'm beyond shocked at how she is treating me. I have never seen this side of her, and it has to be for the first time since I've seen her in ten years. What a great start.

I turn to Grandpa. "I love you and I'll be over to visit soon. When I get out I'm staying with Ryker and Christine." he lowers his eyes for a few moments and pats my hand. He tells me he understands and they both gather their things to leave. I kiss Grandpa goodbye and watch Grandma stop at the door. She looks back at me, her eyes red. I look deep into them, hoping for an explanation to burst out of her. She turns her body and pushes herself down the quiet hallway instead.

"I'll call, Grandpa," I say, trying not to cry. My throat burns with frustration. "I promise. It won't be for long, she will break eventually. Everything will be okay."

"Orca, everything will be okay." Grandpa repeats. I hear a shuffle of bags and clunking of boots against the tiles. Ryker walks up to Grandpa with his hands full of Chinese takeout bags. Ryker looks over at me with a quick smile and Grandpa lets him through. Ryker sets the bags on the small table near my bed and straightens out.

"Hey, Pops!" Ryker smiles at Grandpa. "I ran into Denise. Is everything okay? Want to join us?" He suggests towards the food.

"No, son, that's alright. She's going out to the car right now and I'm going to meet her. I'll see both of you soon." Grandpa gives me a sad yet assuring smile and I wave slightly. He closes the door behind him and Ryker stares at me.

"What was that?" he asks.

"I'll explain soon enough. I don't really feel like talking right now."

He nods slowly with suspicion. He sits down next to me and puts his arm around. I lean into him. "I'm sorry, Orchid."

"Everything is alright. Is it okay if I stay with you and

Christine for a while when I get out of here?"

"Is that really a question?"

I smile lightly. "Thanks."

Ryker pats my back and stands back up. "For the time being, let's chow down."

We both set up plates full of fried rice, chicken teriyaki sticks, and crab rangoon. Ryker sits in the chair and eats off of the small table and I sit on the bed with my food in my lap. It is warm and comforting on my legs.

Maria comes in to check on us and notices our galore of food.

"Sick of hospital food?" Maria laughs.

Ryker nods with his mouth full of fried rice. I take a bite of crab rangoon and smile up at her.

"Join us," Ryker offers. "You have done a lot for Orchid and the least I can do is feed you a decent meal."

"Well, it is my dinner break at the moment. . . ," Maria's accent rolls off of her tongue as her words trail.

"An extra spot?" she points to the bed.

I pat the bed and she brings the small table over closer. I make a plate for her and she digs into the rice. She looks up at us, her cheeks full, and smiles. "The first meal I had when I first came to America is Chinese takeout, surprisingly enough. Very good."

Ryker and I nod our heads with agreement.

"Grandparents come visit you yet?" Maria asks. I'm not super hungry anymore. I nod my head and stab at a pea with my fork.

"Go well?"

I shrug. "It is what it is,"

Ryker eats more slowly and listens to our conversation. I look up at his gaze and it is assuring.

"My grandparents and I don't get along too well, either," Maria says. "No worries. Sometimes certain relations aren't always manageable."

I pick at my rice some more. "That's true."

We all finish eating and Maria checks her watch.

"Back to work I go," she says. "Let me check your

temperature, blood, and medication chart."

I allow her to do all of those and she pulls out some more ibuprofen and a lollipop out of her pocket. "You're one of the best patients I've had."

I smile up at her and she pats my shoulder. "You know where I am if you need me."

She smiles at Ryker and thanks him for dinner once again and hands him a lollipop too. She closes the door behind her.

I help Ryker clean up the table and throw our trash away. I take the ibuprofen and rip open the lollipop. Familiar sweetness invades my tongue.

"A Tootsie pop," I say.

He opens his and sucks on it. The sucker forms a bulge in the side of his cheek. "How many licks do you think it will take to get to the center?"

"I'm not sure. The taste of these remind me of my childhood, though." I must sound unsure because Ryker retorts with: "That's a good thing."

We eat our lollipops and sit in silence. I look out of the window and the sky is starting to fade into a burnt sienna.

"Let's see if there is anything decent on," Ryker suggests. I scoot over in the bed and make room for him. He lays next to me and we make ourselves comfortable. He smells like cologne and musk.

He flicks through the channels and clicks on one.

"Does *That 70's Show* sound alright?" he asks.

"Which seventies show?" I ask.

"No, that's what it's called. *That 70's Show*."

"Ohhhh," I reply.

"The brunette is Jackie, the redhead is Donna, the weird foreign one is Fez, the guy every girl swoons over is Kelso—his real name is Michael but they sometimes call him Kelso—the dude with the afro is Hyde, and the super skinny dude that's dating Donna is Eric."

"Sounds like an interesting show with an interesting crowd of people."

"There's a marathon going on right now. Want to watch it?"

"Why not."

We spend the rest of the night watching television. It

keeps my mind off of things for a while and I enjoy Ryker's company. I watch his mouth turn up as he chuckles at Fez's actions and the butterflies in my stomach roar. His smile is a smile that has never faded from my memory, I'm sure. As a child his cheeks were pudgier, but his smile is still the exact same as it unfolds his beautiful personality.

For once in a very long time, I feel safe and secure. I fall asleep against his arm, his smile engraved deep into my heart.

THE SOUND OF RAIN

Chapter Thirteen

Strong, muscular hands grab at me. Water is flying around me in the air. Loud booms synchronize with the two strong, veiny, dirty hands that grasp at my head and neck. Red streaks my vision as I look up at the sky, and then gold, and then evergreen; they all burn the dark moon and clouds with foggy splashes of color.

Glow.

The hands glow under the booming lights and stars, and I feel their warm, sweaty grip ease. Shock consumes me as their fingertips caress my forehead gently. . . .

****

I wake up and the bed is empty. I sit up and yawn, still not quite used to seeing the morning glow.

Glow.

I furrow my eyebrows at the dream. This one was rather pleasant compared to the other ones. I sit up further and rub my face, realizing it's puffiness is nearly completely gone. Maria's tactic worked.

I look over at the bedside table and see a note:

"Went into the shop today—will be back later this afternoon to bring food and visit."

—*Ryker*

I yawn again as I make my way to the bathroom. I shower and brush my teeth and put on a light blue T-shirt and a pair of ripped jeans. I find a pair of clean, folded hospital socks on the sink and put them on, too. Maria walks in and I order my normal iced coffee and a bowl of yogurt with fruit. She puts hair oil in my hair for me and she offers me some ibuprofen like usual but I refuse. I'm starting to feel a little normal again.

"A couple of doctors, including Dr. Gregor, are going to come in a little bit to run some tests and interview you," Maria says as she writes my order down. "They won't be intervening or hurting you or anything in case you're wondering that."

I chuckle and shake my head. "That's alright, I understand their procedure. Thank you for looking out for me."

"I'd never let anyone hurt you, sweet girl."

This almost moves me to tears.

I hug her and thank her. She tells me she will bring the food in very shortly.

As I wait, I clean up the room a bit: I make my bed, clean up the bathroom, put my dirty clothes in one of the bags that Ryker brought and fold and put away the clean clothes that are left in another bag, and change the garbage and set it outside of the room for one of the hospital janitors to pick up.

Maria brings the food in after a while and sits with me as she checks my temperature and blood pressure like usual. "Your blood pressure is back to its complete normalcy," she says. "So is your temperature. How does your body feel? Any more pain?"

"Physically, there is no more pain," I reply. I take a bite of yogurt.

"Do you feel a different
pain?" I nod.

"Pain helps us learn. It helps us remember." Maria pats my back comfortingly and leaves.

****

After a while, Dr. Gregor comes in with two other female doctors and another male doctor. Dr. Gregor doesn't truly introduce me to them, just as doctors, no more and no less. They examine my eyes—and as cheesy as it is— that's the only physical thing they examine. They then take me to a room to perform a CAT scan.

"This is your third one," Dr. Gregor says. "Technically your first one awake."

I'm not sure how I feel about that but I move on and cooperate.

After the CT scan—which was fairly quick but felt like hours with mumbling doctor talk—Dr. Gregor and I went back to my room and he said I was free to leave and that he contacted my grandparents.

"My grandparents aren't really in the picture anymore," I say, sitting down on the bed.

"On your own already?"

"I guess."

"Ryker still around?"

"Yeah, he's at the shop. He should be here soon to pick me up."

"If you ever need help you can always contact me and the hospital in general. I always tell my patients this to allow them to have a safe place to come to when they need it. Oathpark Medical Center is always here for the community, especially young teens like you."

"Like me?"

"Those who need help finding their way around life."

"Definitely me."

Dr. Gregor smiles and pats my back. He gives me a card from the staff—a normal tradition with their acclaimed favorite patients—and leaves.

Ryker walks in not too long after Dr. Gregor leaves with two strawberry smoothies from the gas station across the street.

"Hey, sweets," I say.

"I heard you can break out now," he sits next to me and hands me a smoothie.

"Thanks. Yeah, I'm ready to go," I say, taking a sip. "Christine knows I'm coming?"

He nods. "She's more excited than I am I think."

I smack his arm lightly. "I'm happy, too. Once I figure things out with Grandma and Grandpa I'll be able to see them again. It isn't even Grandpa, it's Grandma. I'm sick of her hiding things from me."

Ryker looks down. "I'm sorry. I packed your bags, by the way. Technically your grandma already did for you but she gave them to me and told me thank you for letting you stay with us."

"It's okay," I say, standing up. "Let's get out of here."

****

Ryker helps me pack up the room and we carry my hospital bags out to the car. I say goodbye to Maria and we tell each other we will see each other again, but I think that people say that all of the time without really meaning it. I guess we will see.

I put on sunglasses before going outside and see Ryker's car. It's dark blue and a bit beat. I open the door and it smells the same—like pine and Ryker.

"So, this is your hot rod?"

"It's my mom's," Ryker says as he gets in. "Mine was done for. You wouldn't have wanted to see the damage it endured. You probably would have started crying." We both buckle in and he pats my leg.

"How would you know? I'm not much of a wimp anymore, Ryker. I think I'm pretty badass."

"Sorry, but since I cried, I'm pretty positive you would have shed some tears, too. I can't tell whether I'm rubbing off on you now or if you're rubbing off on me." I roll my eyes and smack his arm.

"Ready for your first official car ride?" Ryker grins. I nod and smile.

He pulls out slowly and everything—the trees, grass, other cars pass by us like melted syrup. Once we get to more busy roads driving away from the hospital the car moves faster and I gasp and squeeze my eyes shut. The feeling is familiar and I breathe; Ryker puts his hand on mine.

"Exhilarating, isn't it?"

"Can we go faster?"

He laughs. "Legally, no."

"You should teach me how to drive."

"I will once you're used to your vision."

"So . . . tomorrow?

"Not that soon; but soon enough."

"Sounds good to me."

I look over at him. His dark hair falls in his face, the summer sun lightening each strand to a shimmering burnt amber and I lean over to push it out of his face as he drives.

He chuckles and reaches for my hand. He holds it up, the warm sun flickering through the windows against the trees reflecting off of both of our hands and kisses it. I smile and lean my head against the window lightly, looking out at my other world while the one I'm with is right next to me.

Ryker's house is small and blue. My heart pounds as I look around his yard, oddly nervous to go inside. Small flower pots sit on the porch steps. He grabs my bags for me and we walk up the steps. As he opens the door, the familiar scent of warmth and fruit greet my nose. A woman sitting on the couch watching television looks up and jumps from her relaxed position quickly. Her golden brown hair sweeps off of her shoulders as she does so.

"Orchid!"

"Christine," I breathe as she hugs me. We squeeze each other hard. "You're beautiful."

Her full lips turn and show her white teeth. Her eyes are blue like Ryker's.

"You're beautifuller," she says,

"Not a real word." Ryker states as he goes into a room in the hallway with my bags.

"Hush, she is. Are you hungry?"

"Not at the moment, thank you." I reply, suddenly shy. It was like I was meeting a completely different person with the same voice.

"Okay. I'll let you settle in. I talked to your grandparents earlier. They both say they love you."

I give her a tight smile and say thank you.

I follow Ryker into the room and it is so plain it

hurts my eyes. The walls are white and the pale yellow bed lays in the middle of the room with a nightstand, a lamp, and a small clock radio. There is a dresser and a large window with gray curtains on the other wall.

"This is the guest bedroom," Ryker says. "Sorry it isn't all that great."

I smile as I look around. "I like it."

He starts unpacking one of my bags and pulls out some of my T-shirts. I look at all of them, a colorful array of band symbols on each.

"Good taste," he says as he puts them away.

"You helped me pick them out," I laugh. I grab a pair of pants and fold them.

After we finish putting everything away, I plop face-first onto the bed.

Ryker sits next to me. "Are you ready to talk about what happened at the hospital?"

I sigh, sit up, and nod my head. "Can we walk around outside? I want to see the park,"

He nods his head and tell Christine we will be back

soon. I grab a jacket and my sunglasses on our way out.

As we walk down the street I see kids riding their bikes. They stare at us—specifically me—as we pass by.

"They know?"

"Everyone knows."

I groan. I pull my glasses and jacket closer to my face and body.

"Don't pay attention to them. Tell me what went down at the hospital."

"I was trying to get Grandma to tell me what happened during the accident when I was a kid."

"And?"

"Barely anything. She told me about my mom and dad and she acted like she was going to mention someone else but she stopped herself. I got mad and told her I didn't want to be around her anymore with her hiding things from me unless she told me."

"Oh," Ryker replies. I look over at him and he looks at the ground as we walk.

"I wish things were different."

"You can see now. Things *are* different."

"I meant with Grandma and Grandpa."

"Oh." he says again. I knew he wasn't going to say anything to me.

I sigh.

Ryker looks over at me and grins as he pulls two rectangular thick pieces of paper from his pocket. "Things are different on Tuesday . . . when we go to see The Rolling Stones!"

"You're kidding!" I say, laughing. "I didn't think you were going through with the idea of going. Coincidence you found a tour date right when I get out of the hospital?"

"You bet I'm not. I've been planning to take you with for a month now, but that's my secret. Let's forget about the world for one day."

I laugh until I'm crying. I wipe my eyes and hug his side. "Sounds good to me."

"But tomorrow, Saturday, we're going to my guitar competition." Ryker grins.

"Yes, we are!"

"Carson will be there but I don't think I'm going to stick around him and his friends anymore."

"If it's because of me, I want you to do what makes you happy."

"Nah, I mean you're part of the reason that made me realize how ignorant he really can be. I'm not sure."

"I'm excited to see you play. What song did you choose?"

"That's a secret."

"Aw, now you're keeping secrets from me? Is it harder doing that now that I can see?" I chuckle.

"Oh, gimme a break. You'll like the song I think, though."

There is a sudden pain in my stomach. I'm tempted to go see Grandma and Grandpa even though we are fighting. "Can we stop by Grandma and Grandpa's house?"

"Are you sure?"

"Yes. I want to see what the house looks like. I want to say hi to Grandpa."

"You got it."

****

We get up to the house and it's foreign structure is oddly familiar to me. I walk up to it slowly and knock on the door three times. Ryker stands next to me.

Grandma stands at the door. She smiles lightly at me. "Hi, honey."

"Hi, Grandma."

"Come in."

We both walk in and the same comforting, vintage scent greets my nose. I try not to give in.

"Is Grandpa home?"

"He's at the shop right now. Do you want something to eat? Something to drink?" I shake my head no as I look around. Grandpa's chair. The dining table. I close my eyes and maneuver my way through over to my dining chair and sit. It's hard wood is still rough on my butt. I open them and get up. I walk over to the shelf with the picture frames and look at all of the smiling faces. All of the pictures consist of:

A beautiful woman in a wedding dress. No groom.

A younger couple which I assume to be Grandma and Grandpa. Grandpa is holding Grandma bridal-style. Grandpa was very handsome.

A picture of Ryker as a child with Christine. They're holding hands and Ryker is sticking his tongue out at her. She's laughing and her young, plump cheeks accentuate her beautiful smile.

A picture of a baby smiling. Probably me.

A picture of the shop when it first opened twenty years ago. Ryker's dad, my grandpa, and Archie are all standing in front of the shop.

And lastly, there is a crumpled piece of paper stuck inside the edge of a frame that is partially broken. In the picture, a small strawberry blond girl smiles. She doesn't have many freckles. Her front tooth is missing.

I inch closer to the girl and the mirror, and I see that her eyes are green and they continuously keep shaking; like she is in a demented trance. Her mouth is partially open, showing a missing front tooth.

I squeeze my eyes shut at the sudden dream flashback.

I furrow my eyebrows and look at Grandma. She is in the kitchen making coffee. I look at Ryker and he turns his head away.

I ignore him and walk down the hall and into my bedroom. Grandma must have cleaned it because everything is made up. The walls are blank and white, except for the purple dream catcher. I smile and walk over to it.

"To catch the bad dreams," Ryker insists. I shrug and thank him for his effort for getting rid of my dreams.

"I like how dream catchers look," I claim. "Very hippieish."

"Indeed. I'll buy you more."

I look further around my room. The blankets are white. Everything is white except for my brown wooden dresser that hold my clothes and the colorful perfume bottles. My old clock radio sits next to my bed. I go over to my bed, sit down, and turn it on.

Gypsy by Fleetwood Mac ripples through the room. "Is your bedroom what you expected?" Ryker's voice greets the back of my head.

"It's nice." I say.

"We need to decorate it now that you can see it."

"Probably not anytime soon." I reply.

I stand up and walk over to the closet. I look through the clothes that hang on the rack casually. Everything feels the same around me. I close my eyes and walk around slowly. I reopen them again.

"I don't feel as comfortable in my room as I did before." I state.

"I think that's just a temporary feeling." Ryker replies.

"I hope so."

I go over to the radio and shut it off. I can't stop thinking about that picture.

"Are you okay?" Ryker asks.

I nod my head. "Yeah. Just still a little out of it, I guess. I wanted to see Grandpa."

"We can stop by the shop if you want."

"No, that's okay. I don't want to get in the way of his work."

That crumpled piece of paper. . . .

"It's up to you. Do you want to go back, then?"

"Who is in that crumpled picture?" I ask.

"What crumpled picture?"

I look up at his face and he genuinely doesn't know what I'm talking about.

"Never mind. We can leave."

We get up and I go say goodbye to Grandma. Even though we are fighting, I still want to be civil.

"Honey please, just come home. Everything is better now. You can see. Your grandpa is happier. He wants you home, too." Grandma pleads.

"It's not better. It's worse. Everything is worse." I claim.

She hugs me and I hug her slightly back. "I want things to be better," I say. "But nothing will change unless I know. You know that. So I'll wait. I'll let you figure things out on your own time and when you want to tell me. I'll let you and Grandpa finish healing from the accident I was just in. But I can't continue to hold a grudge on this anymore. I can't hold a grudge on you."

Grandma doesn't say anything. She knows she is defeated.

I kiss her cheek and move towards the door. I look back at her and she is back in the kitchen. I look over at the shelf with the pictures and grab the crumpled photo of the girl and walk out of the door without looking back.

THE SOUND OF RAIN

Chapter Fourteen

I wake up to the sound of Ryker's guitar blaring in the basement.

I groan and rub my eyes. I roll over on the bed and stuff my pillow over my ears. I try to go back to sleep for a little while longer but his guitar is so loud it's vibrating my bed sheets. I'm surprised Christine hasn't screamed at him yet . . . maybe she has but he probably didn't hear her at all.

After about ten miserable minutes, I finally kick the covers off of me and go into the bathroom. The house is on the verge of freezing and I realize that Ryker and Christine are eskimos in the summer heat. I shiver as I look in the mirror.

I haven't looked in the mirror genuinely since I was in the hospital. I sigh and lean my cheek in my palm and stare at myself. I have bags underneath my green eyes and they're puffy from sleep. I wash my face with cold water and Christine's face wash and pat my skin dry. I apply face moisturizer (courtesy of Christine again) and comb through my hair. I look in the mirror and I look normal. Pretty, even. Sort of.

I look through the cabinets slightly and find a tube of mascara. I twist it open slowly and study the dark fibers on its wand. I step closely to the mirror and comb the mascara brush through my eyelashes carefully.

Red eyes stare back at me.

I gasp slightly and pull away from the mirror.

I sigh and apply mascara on the other eye quickly and brush my teeth.

I hustle back into my room and get dressed. My ears are used to Ryker's loud guitar by now, but after I get dressed, I run down the stairs and peek through the basement door frame. His back is towards me and his strong arms are intertwined with his guitar. He's wearing a black sweatshirt and jeans. I watch him walk around the room and play for a few moments before he stops by his guitar amp and unplugs it.

"Come on out."

I smile lightly feeling oddly defeated and creep my way through the door frame.

He looks up at me as he's fidgeting with the plug and smiles. "Morning, Sleeping Beauty."

I walk over to him. "It was a beautiful sleep before you ruptured my eardrums."

He pulls me to him and cups my ears between his hands gently and studies my face. "Are you wearing makeup?"

"Yeah . . . does it look bad?" I look into his blue eyes.

"No."

"Okay."

"You're beautiful."

"You're beautifuller, ocean eyes."

He smirks. "Not a real word."

"My eyes are green but I don't know what type of green."

"I'll find out and I'll let you know. How can I make it up to you for almost rupturing your eardrums?" I blush and laugh. I put my hands up to his over my ears. "Make me breakfast?"

He scoffs. "I had something else in mind, buuut. . . ," I lean up and kiss him and he tastes like mint and clean laundry. I pull away after a few moments and hug him.

"Has your mom screamed at you already?"

"For playing the guitar?"

"Yeah," I chuckle.

"What kind of question is that? Of course she has."
I laugh and kiss him again. I pull away to go over to
look at his guitars but his grip on me is too tight. He
kisses me multiple times until I'm cracking up and my
cheeks hurt. "Which one is the one that I usually play?"

"The blue one." he says as he kisses the side of my
mouth.

I walk over and pick it up. The weight of it is the
same.

"Do you still want to learn?" Ryker asks.

I nod. "After your competition, though. I want to
make sure your attention is completely on that."

"Fair enough." he plops down on the couch next to
me. I pat his forearm comfortingly.

"It's nice being able to see." I state quietly.

"Of course it is."

"I have a lot of catching up to do."

"Not much has changed, honestly, Orchid."

"Catching up with the world, I mean. I want to see the whole wide world."

"I'll make sure we travel a lot once I become the biggest rockstar known in Oathpark, Florida. Well, hopefully by then I'll be big enough where my name will used like a cuss-word."

I laugh. "I'll appreciate that very much. I appreciate you."

"I appreciate you for appreciating me."

I smile slightly and look down at my hands. "What are we, Ryker?"

"What do you mean?"

"Like, us. We've been friends for a very long time and now we seem like we are something more."

"Whatever you want. I'll say this, though: everything came naturally. We act like this naturally and I think that's the best part of our relationship."

I laugh and put my hand on his cheek as I stand up.

"I like that. C'mon, Joey Donner, I'm hungry."

"Joey Donner?" he asks as we walk up the stairs.

"From *10 Things I Hate About You.*"

"Still doesn't ring a bell."

"We watched the movie together when it first came out in theatres."

"Well, I did. You didn't."

"Apparently you didn't either since you have no clue who the hell I'm talking about."

We walk up into the kitchen and Ryker decides that we should go into Daisy Doughnuts for breakfast.

"This July heat is really killing me," Ryker complains as we walk out of the door.

"Yeah. I like it when it cools off a bit in the fall. It's still pretty warm here but at least we aren't having a heat stroke."

We get into the air-conditioned car and all of the town's shops are lined up close together like books on a bookshelf. Very convenient.

We walk into Daisy Doughnuts and the walls are strawberry milk-pink and the tables are cream. An old woman is at the front glass counter and she is talking to a young woman with an apron. We inch closer to the glass counter and it's lined with colorful doughnuts. They are all glazed with every color of the rainbow and they look too pretty to eat. The sprinkles are mesmerizing as their constellations of pastel colors lay perfectly still on top of the sugary glaze.

The old woman's voice breaks me from my trance. "Orchid Thomas," she smiles, her wrinkles showing predominantly. "Long time, no see."

I look up and smile back at her. "Hi, Mrs. Nessle." "Call me Daisy already! You never call me Daisy and everyone else calls me Daisy."

I laugh. "Hi, Daisy. These doughnuts look way too pretty to eat." "These ones are definitely eye candy, aren't they? You won't regret eating them, though. How are you feeling, honey?"

"I'm feeling good. I'm happy."

"What about your honey?" she looks over at Ryker, who is sampling a Moon Pie doughnut.

He turns around a smiles sheepishly, his mouth full of doughnut. "Good."

"A medium box of doughnuts, on the house. Take it as a welcome-back gift." Daisy grins. Her dark pink lips are smooth and they contrast with her silky white bob that frames her face.

I try to protest, but she practically shoves the box in my arms. I laugh and shake my head.

"That chocolate one with the pink cream cheese frosting looks pretty good. Or the grape jelly one with the bright green glaze."

"Pick them."

Ryker takes a strip of paper towel that sits on top of the counter and grabs them. I pick out a couple of different colorful flavors and we go and sit in a cream-colored booth. The seats are lined with green velvet.

"I love it in here," I say with a mouth-full of chocolate ganache.

"It's very . . . interesting to say the least. Talking with your mouth full is rude, Orc."

I stick my tongue out. Ryker has a glob of pink frosting on his cheek and I wish I had a camera.

"I really want a camera." I claim outside of my head.

"Cameras are sold everywhere. I'll buy you one."

"I want it to capture the world."

"Doesn't surprise me."

We finish eating our doughnuts and take the rest back to the house where Christine eats two. Later in the afternoon, Ryker goes back to playing his guitar in the basement and I hang out with Christine on the porch. The air is bearable and the sky isn't blue anymore.

"I'm glad you're here, Orchid."

"I'm glad, too."

She swings gently on the porch bench. She's barefoot and her toenails are dark purple. "I'm glad you're finally able to live life the way you're supposed to."

"If this never happened, I think I would have been just fine in this world."

"I know, baby. I'm just saying. I think everyone should always have a chance at change if they're able to grasp it. If not, they can still live their life just fine."

"How do you think this happened?"

"With you being able to see all of a sudden?"

I nod.

"God has his ways."

I shrug. I should've known that was coming. I decide to change the subject. "I think I need to re-learn how to read."

She smiles and goes into the house. A few moments later she plops back onto the porch bench with a book in her hand and pats the seat next to her.

I sit next to her and she opens the book in my lap. It's thick and I try to look at the cover to see what book it is but I almost one-hundred-percent probably won't know anyways.

"When I point to a word, I'll say it and I want you to repeat it."

I nod.

We read the first two chapters of whatever book Christine grabbed before Ryker interrupts us by rushing out of the house with his guitar.

"Competition starts in ten minutes! Hustle!" Ryker shouts. Christine and I rush to get our sandals and we both hop into the car. Christine kicks Ryker out of the driver's seat and we drive off with the windows down, the echoes of the announcers and summer air blowing through my hair.

****

When we get there, Christine and I go find a spot to sit. I don't see Grandma or Grandpa around. I wish I could see Grandpa.

Ryker kisses me on the cheek quickly and I wish him good-luck. He rushes towards the back of the stage area. The Oathpark park has a few tents set up around for food and drinks and on the other side of the park the market is going on. There is a stage in the middle near the dock and there are a few tech-people setting the amps up. The stage lights make the water glisten red, yellow, and green.

Christine and I find a bench that is near the stage and sit. I offer to go get us drinks and Christine hands me a five dollar bill. I make my way over to a striped yellow tent where two men stand talking. One of them is wearing a police uniform.

"Orchid Jane." the man in the police uniform greets,

his voice familiar.

"Officer Dean." I smile. He is tall and his hair is dirty-blond and thick. His face is strong and he has a sharp jawline. He has a few wrinkles but still looks young.

"How are you feeling?"

"Decent. I'm here for Ryker."

"I figured. Your grandparents miss you."

I roll my eyes. Seriously, when can I not be reminded about my grandparents or God? "I know."

"You seem upset."

"Yeah." I brush past him and go up to the guy who is serving drinks. "Can I get two Cokes, please?"

"You don't have to be upset with me."

"I am, Officer Dean. I am upset. I'm upset because I just got into a car accident with my best friend where I was put in the hospital for almost a full week and I come out of the hospital, suddenly able to see, and everyone thinks I'm a freak. I'm mad because no-one will tell me what the hell is going on, what the hell *has* been going on with my past, or who the hell is roaming the streets of our town. I'm upset because everyone keeps saying the only reason why this happened is because of "God's work", but if this was all "God's work", He would be helping me. He wouldn't have let any of this happen. And, most of all, I'm upset because you and your 'partners in crime' won't do anything. If something happens tonight, Officer Dean, if something happens to any of these people tonight, I hope you take all of the blame."

I feel a nudge on my arm and the drink guy is holding out the two Cokes I ordered. I thank him, give him two dollars, and look back at Officer Dean. He gives me a disappointed tight smile and looks away.

I sit next to Christine and hand her one of the Cokes. She looks around at the water and the people walking by and she seems happy. I lean back and open my Coke. I take a drink and put the can against my forehead. The coolness of the aluminum feels good against my hot, frustrated face.

"I'm so excited to finally see him play," Christine states.

"I am, too."

Christine laughs. "Ryker has such a gift and I'm

finally able to see him share it with the world. Or with the town for the moment being. Soon enough he will be playing venue after venue, just like The Rolling Stones."

"We are going to see The Rolling Stones on Tuesday."

"I know. I wanted to come with but Ryker said I'd be a buzz-kill."

"I think he deserves a smack in the face for that. I'll keep you in mind."

"After that smack back at the shop, I think he will be covered for a few more mistakes."

I look down at my hands nervously. "Oh, Ryker told you about that, huh?"

"Yeah. He was telling me he deserved it, though. He never told me the reason why but I'll leave that between you two."

I take an awkward sip of my Coke and I hear a pitchy thud on stage. "Yeah. Hey, I think they're getting started."

The lights move on the stage as an old man in a suit walks up the steps and in front of the microphone. I assume he is the Mayor.

"Can I get everyone's attention, please?"

The audience begins to quiet down to a hush.

"Tonight, Oathpark will be hosting its eighth Summer Nights Guitar & Musician Competition. As usual, the market will be on the other side of the park." A few claps interrupt.

"Despite recent events, I'd like to thank everyone in this community for holding each other together for as long as possible. Orchid Thomas, are you out there, sweetheart?"

My heart stops. I gasp and inch closer to Christine, who is giggling.

"Ah, I see you over there on the bench!" the Mayor states with a grin. "Orchid, I'd like to wish you well and that we are all here for you. Your dear friend, Ryker, who is playing tonight, has been remarkable and I'd like to give a very special round of applause for him. C'mon!"

A roaring wave of hands sharply clapping together stings my ears. All of the fake claps burn every inch of my ear drums and I want to scream. Reality isn't here and it never will be in Oathpark, apparently. My face is so hot it's almost numb.

"Alright, that's enough emotional-talk for the night. Let's get on with the show! First up, Carson Glenfield with his band, 'Wicked Cigarettes'!"

Another roar of clapping. I clap slowly.

Carson walks on stage and I stare. His hair is long, bleach-blonde, and he's wearing a dark-blue T-shirt that accentuate his muscles. He's alright for looks, but Ryker is definitely cuter and not a piece of shit.

Carson starts the song out lightly, but after a few moments of light guitar strokes, the other three members start slamming their instruments pretty hard.

"Yikes," Christine says.

I nod in agreement. "Yikes, indeed."

After what seems like a lot longer than three minutes, the Mayor comes back on stage and claps roughly. "Alright, that was Wicked Cigarettes! Pretty heavy there, boys. Rock N' roll, am I right? Yow!" the Mayor makes a rock-on hand symbol.

Crickets—I hear them.

"Okay, next up, we have Ruby Fitzgerald and The Red Suns!"

As three girls with bright red hair and black fishnets walk out on stage, Christine tells me she is going to go and get a sandwich.

"Do you want anything?"

"No thank you." I smile.

"Okay, I'll be right back." she pats my shoulder and walks off into the lights and tents.

I look over to see if Officer Dean is still here. I feel kind of guilty for what I said. I feel like everything I said was true, but I still feel like crap for actually saying it.

I sit and listen to Ruby and The Red Suns. I kind of like their music—it's edgy with a light-hearted twist. Plus, their fashion sense isn't half bad. They sing about heartbreak and loneliness and I'm not sure if I connect with that completely relationship-wise, but it's still relatable. I tap my leg with the beat.

Christine comes back with not a sandwich, but a camera. I ask her where she went.

"Oh, I got a sandwich. I was so hungry I ate it in one bite. Let me take your picture."

"Where did you get the camera?" I ask as she ruffles my hair up a bit and smooths my shoulders.

"I asked Bill from Oathpark News Printing if I could borrow it to take a picture of you," she looks closer into my eyes. "Are you wearing mascara?"

I smile shyly and nod. I lean against the back of the bench and hold my arm up on my crossed knee. I smile wide.

"Cheese!"

The bright flash makes me wince. I hope she was still able to take a decent picture, though.

"Okay, one more and then I'll try to see if someone else will take our picture together."

I sit cross-legged on the bench this time and look up at her. A suddenly pressure against my shoulder and side makes me turn and gasp.

"Smile for the picture, ya weirdo," Ryker says tightly as he smiles. I laugh and wrap my arms around his neck and playfully press my smiling face against his.

"Aw you guys are too sweet," Christine says. "Ryker,

what the hell are you doing down here? You're going up I think after the Ruby chicks."

"Mom, it's Ruby and The Red Suns," he claims. "And I know, I just went to grab a bottle of water and say you guys taking pictures. I'll see you soon. Want me to take a picture of you and Orchid?"

"Yes, if you would be so kind."

Ryker take the camera and Christine sits next to me. I smile once more and the flash doesn't hurt as bad this time.

"Alright, hustle, Feldspar."

"Bye, Mama." Ryker kisses Christine on the cheek and squeezes my shoulder quickly as he jogs off.

Bill walks over and Christine ands him the camera. He tells me welcome back and I say thank you like a polite person. I'm anxious to see Ryker play now and I wish he would because my stomach is getting tied in knots all of a sudden.

Ruby and The Red Suns finish and we all clap. The Mayor pushes through a crowd of people to get back on the stage and he's wearing a white bib-like cloth around his neck and there is some type of meat sauce that stains the corner of his mouth. The cloth bib is clearly useless because there is also a stain on the front of his suit.

"Ruby and The Red Suns, everyone! Before I announce the next act, I must say to you over there, Gerry in the meat tent, those ribs are absolutely remarkable! Mmm." he licks his lips. Charming. "Up next, we have a solo act—Ryker Feldspar and his guitar!"

A man with headphones runs up the steps and hands the Mayor a piece of paper.

"Oops—Ryker Feldspar and his guitar, Lucy Diamond!"

I laugh and clap. "Come on, Ryker." I press my hands together tightly. Christine grips my knee and the biggest smile is plastered up her cheeks.

Ryker strides out on the stage and hooks up his guitar. He sits on a chair and the holes in his jeans makes him look oddly cute. Before he plays, he tunes the guitar for a minute or two and takes a deep breath. He looks at me. I smile and give him two thumbs up. He gives me a small smirk and begins strumming slightly.

The beat amplifies and I've heard this song before— the guitar, the way the song starts slow. There is music and a male voice rings through my ears. Ryker isn't singing—he's strumming along with the guy singing on some sort of CD.

CD.

"Lynyrd Skynyrd!" I exclaim. I laugh.

"Unbelievable." I clap my hands.

Christine yells over the crowd. "He said you'd like this."

The song grows more intense as the chorus comes up and Ryker stands up. He walks around the stage playing Lucy, and everyone in the crowd is cheering. I'm so mesmerized I don't even notice.

After a few moments, the song speeds up even more and Ryker slides on his knees for the guitar solo. I jumping up and down screaming, laughing, and crying. He is *amazing*. His face is sweaty and scrunched up with concentration as his hands grip and slash the guitar.

As the song finishes, Ryker sits back on the chair and drinks his water bottle as this whole crowd is basically worshipping and screaming his name. He looks so content. He looks at me. I look at Christine and she's sobbing her damn eyes out. I hug her tightly and we sway.

Ryker goes back behind the stage and there is still cheering when the

Mayor comes up to announce the next person. "Wow, oh wow. Lynyrd Skynyrd really takes me back. That guitar solo—you nailed it, Feldspar! One more round of applause!"

The crowd goes nuts again. I clap until my hands are stinging and my ears are ringing. Ryker comes out finally and he grins as people fist-bump him and clap him on the back of his shoulders. He jogs up to me and I jog up to him and we collide and I give him the biggest hug I could ever give. He picks me up and spins me around and I'm laughing so hard because I'm so proud of him I'm basically crying.

"My baby! Ryker, I'm so proud of you!" Christine hugs both of us.

"Thanks, Mom. I love you. I love you both." I hug him tighter and the next act starts. We all sit down for a bit and listen to a man named Donald Klebann who plays folk music. It's light and good recovery music.

Ryker stands up. "Let's go by the water for a few minutes."

Ryker's mom tells us she's going to go talk to a friend of hers and that she will be back. Ryker tells her that we are going to walk around for a few minutes.

I get up and follow him and we go to the dock that is the farthest from the stage. The music dims until all I'm able to hear are crickets. The moon is out and the light creates white strands in the dark water that float and glisten. Ryker and I sit on the edge of the dock and take our shoes off and stick our feet in the cool water. We are silent and it's nice.

"I'm very proud of you."

"I'm glad."

"You remember that? The CD?"

"Of course. How could I forget Kyle—"

"Dunnell-dweeb." we both say at the same time. We laugh.

"Yeah."

"How long did you practice that for? That was perfect."

"A while."

"A while?"

"A while, as in while you were in the hospital."

I smile lightly and pat his hand. "Thanks for being there." He smiles lightly and looks out at the moon and the water. The darkness accentuates his jawline and I kiss it lightly. He wraps his arms around me and pulls me into his lap. I laugh and lean my head into his neck and we sit like that for a while until we hear crunches of grass behind us. I whip my head around and a bright flashlight clicks in my eyes. I gasp and burrow my face into Ryker's neck again.

"Officer Dean?" Ryker asks. No answer.

I slide off of Ryker and stand on my knees. I face the light and put my arm up to block most of the brightness but not completely.

"Who are you?" I ask. No answer.

Ryker's voice pierces my ears with an edge. "Who the fuck are you? Answer me, or I'll—" the light turns off and fast footsteps pace the grass away from us.

I turn my head, get up quickly, and jolt towards the running figure.

"Coward! Come back here and show yourself!" I yell as I run. My lungs burn and Ryker is behind me yelling my name. "Come back here and show yourself!"

I feel a grip on my arm and it whips me back. I fall backwards into the grass and I lay there panting. Ryker is next to me. "It's okay. He's gone."

I nod slightly and put my arm over my face. My lungs really hurt. "Are you okay?" he asks. I nod again.

"Just . . . not used . . . to running."

He chuckles and puts a hand on my forehead.

We lay for a minute or two longer until my breathing calms and he helps me up. We walk arm-in-arm together back to the competition. Ryker got second place in the competition and Ruby and The Red Suns got first. I think the whole system is rigged—which doesn't surprise me in Oathpark—and he gets a fifty-dollar check. The three of us go home together. Ryker and I don't talk about what happened.

THE SOUND OF RAIN

Chapter Fifteen

On Tuesday morning, the sun beams milky white through the gray curtains and dims the yellow blanket that I'm tangled in. The quiet morning air is unorthodox to my ears and they ring. I didn't have a dream last night. The flashlight.

I rub my eyes and groan.

I stretch and go out into the living room to find Ryker sitting quietly on the couch, still in his pajamas, reading a magazine. He looks up at me and smiles.

"Good morning," he says.

I sit next to him on the couch and lean my legs on his. He pats the top of my foot.

"Morning." I kiss him on the cheek and Christine walks out of the hallway, yawning. Her pajama bottoms are purple and her hair is still pretty, even from a full night of sleep.

"Alright, no PDA while I'm in here please. It's too early,"

"Ma, it was a kiss on the cheek. Not porn."

She winks at me and turns back to Ryker. "I was just kidding. You're making Orchid and I breakfast." Ryker rolls his eyes as he stands up to go into the kitchen.

Christine gives him a side hug as he walks by her. "Love you my sweet boy."

He pats her on the head and tells her he loves her, too. I smile and follow them.

After breakfast—Ryker's infamous eggs and bacon that Christine loves and now so do I—Ryker and I pack snacks, money, and an extra pair of clothes in case they're needed. We leave mid-afternoon and kiss Christine goodbye.

"Be safe and have fun! No doing drugs! If I find out you're doing drugs, I'm murdering both of you!" Christine calls out to us.

"I'll call when we get there," Ryker shouts out of the driver's window as we pull out of the driveway. Ryker turns the radio on and Mick Jagger croons out of his car speakers.

"The best classic example of rock and roll," Ryker beats the steering wheel with his hands. He rolls the windows down and warm air whips the hair around our faces. I watch out of the window: golden cornfields and green stalks blend together like an oil painting. Behind the cornfield is the other end of lake that is farthest from the park. Another lonely dock sits next to it with a couple of tattered, old houses.

Fire burns the cornfield to a crisp.

I gasp at the sudden flash of fire across my vision.

The women crawling, clawing at me.

We pass the cornfield quickly and I crane my head towards the back window to stare at the field for a few seconds longer. It's empty and the way it sways with the wind gives me goosebumps.

"What's wrong?" Ryker asks over The Rolling Stones. I lean back in my seat normally and put my head back. I close my eyes. "Nothing."

****

We wait in line with a ton of other people to get into the venue. Ryker leaves me alone for a second as he calls Christine on the pay phone across the street of the venue. The air is warm and it smells like cologne and cheap alcohol; a very familiar scent.

Ryker comes back and we go through the security where they check our bodies and bags quickly. The venue is huge - we are on the field ground of the concert arena but there are millions of seats everywhere around us. We find a spot and lay the old blanket we brought with us down and set our bag of food and drinks down beside us. The venue is playing a multitude of different bands as we wait for the stadium to fill up: Fleetwood Mac, then the Goo Goo Dolls, and additionally Aerosmith echo throughout the windy space. I lay back on the blanket and watch the sunset as Ryker opens a bottle of Coke. A couple behind us with thick, stringy hair smell like weed and some type of herbal fruit tea.

"I love your peachy locks," the girl with beaded dreads and a distressed shirt says.

"Thank you," I smile. I rarely get compliments from random people. Or, I never got them when I was blind.

"I like your dreadlocks."

"Thanks."

The girl's assumed boyfriend scoots closer to us and she follows. He extends a strong hand out to Ryker. "James." Ryker gives him a small smile and shakes his hand firmly. "Ryker."

The girl joins in, too: "My name is Jewel."

"That's a pretty name," I state. "My name is Orchid."

"I love it." Jewel smiles.

"Where are you guys from?" Ryker asks. It's obvious that they're not from Oathpark; especially with the weed aroma.

"Dew City—it's about two hours north of Oathpark." James states.

"Wow, you guys drove for that long?" I ask.

James pats Jewel's shoulder and smiles. "We are always up for an adventure."

Jewel looks at me for a few moments with scrunched eyebrows and asks: "Wait, aren't you that girl that was blind or something?"

Aw, no.

"Uh, yeah, I am," I say awkwardly. "The news is really covering everything, aren't they?"

"Yeah," James says. "It doesn't bother us though. We think that's pretty damn magical."

I sigh with relief and laugh lightly. "Yeah. Magical,

if that's what you want to call it."

"The dude that hit you guys looks pretty damaged. Physically and mentally." Jewel makes a disgusted face.

"Do you have a picture of the guy who hit us?"

"I do, actually," James pulls a crumpled piece of gray paper out of his back pocket.

"Can I see it?" I ask. My heart is pounding.

James hands it to me and I brace myself before looking. Ryker leans over my shoulder as I unravel the paper from its wrinkles.

The man's mugshot is typical. He has light hair, but due to the grayscale of the photo, I can't tell what his actual hair color is and eye color. He has a very slim face and somewhat pouty lips. He has a dark hair shadow that makes his cheeks look very sunken in. His eyes are large and almond-shaped. Ryker pulls away from my shoulder and looks at James and Jewel without saying anything. I look up. "How come no one will catch him? How is it this hard to catch anybody?" I remember the confrontation I had with Officer Dean. I still feel a little guilty.

"I think it's because of how he commits the crimes.

He is able to flee really easily." Jewel says.

"Maybe. . . ." I state. I hand the photo back to James.

"Anyway, enough negative stuff. Where are you guys from?" James asks.

"Oathpark," I state.

"Neat." Jewel states.

I nod and smile. The only difference though is that the smile is fabricated because I can't stop thinking about the picture. James and Ryker continue to talk and Jewel and I lie down on the blanket next to each other on our backs. I tell her a little bit about myself and vice versa. She jots down her number and gives it to me and I stick it in my pocket, happy that I've made a new friend.

I sit back up after a while, the sun almost completely engulfed by the dark blue summer night sky. The stadium is loud now; so loud I can barely hear the venue music playing anymore. A sudden guitar starts and a smaller band that is opening for The Rolling Stones called The RaiderZ run out. They all had long hair that blew graciously in the wind. I like their vibe.

Ryker and I stand up as everyone starts screaming and jumping. We do the same—not as hardcore because my head is still fragile—but I think I'm having fun if this is what true fun feels like.

The RaiderZ play more songs for an hour or so and there is a fifteen minute transition period to prepare for The Rolling Stones. We both sit down under the bright stage lights and I watch the small bugs floating around them like a cloud of stardust. I look over at Ryker and everything seems like it's in slow motion as I stare at him. His teeth are straight and his smile is so wide, so genuine, it makes tear up. His brown shaggy hair is damp with sweat. The colored lights around us glisten a rainbow on his face and his eyes glitter. I lean over and wrap my arms around his sweaty neck. He wraps his around my torso.

"Thank you," I say loudly in his ear.

"No need to thank me."

"I'm thanking you. You deserve more than a thank you. You deserve the world."

"I only need you and Mom."

I smile and stare into the oceans that are his eyes. They glisten.

"Chartreuse," he states loudly over the music.

"What?"

"I found the right green. Chartreuse." his smile is wide.

I laugh and kiss his warm cheek and more guitar strings zip through my ears. We both stand up again, holding each other's sweaty hands, and sway with Mick Jagger's voice.

James yells: "Lovebirds!" in our ears behind us and we laugh.

I look behind me and Jewel and James are hugging, too.

This hot summer night is filled with buzzing warmth, a sky full of echoing music that shake the stars, and a everlasting comfort that I can't ever forget. I kiss Ryker under these stars, the screaming people, The Rolling Stones, and the lights that flash against our sweaty foreheads and lips.

I feel the music blaring, vibrating in my chest and it vibrates with the love that is consuming my heart. It vibrates; it lives. I'm still here. I can see. I won't leave again.

THE SOUND OF RAIN

Chapter Sixteen

Before we get into the car, we say goodbye to Jewel and James and I tell Jewel I'll call her sometime tomorrow. Ryker calls Christine at the payphone across the street to tell her we are on our way home. It's chilly out now and there are a lot of people standing around us smoking cigarettes and other foreign herbs. I wrap the blanket around me.

"Wait, what the fuck?"

I look over at him. I scrunch my eyebrows. *What?*

He holds his finger up. "Mom, slow down. Okay, we will be home as soon as we can. Okay, love you, hang in there. Bye."

We get in the car quickly and I ask what's wrong. "Mom said there was someone throwing rocks at her window and your grandparents' windows. A few other houses around ours too were getting vandalized but she's scared."

"Did it stop?"

"She said right now it has. But she said it's like the

dude is walking around in a fucking circle chucking rocks at the same people's houses." he starts the car and backs out of the parking space. We race down the road and he merges onto the highway. I wrap the blanket around me tighter and watch the streetlights whip past us like orange smears of frosting against the dark sky.

"Everything is okay," Ryker assures me.

"I know." I look over at him. My stomach begins to hurt and I ignore it.

"I had fun."

"So did I."

He smiles, the streetlights changing position on his face as we move. The shadows contour his face and he's handsome. Ever since I've been able to see I can't stop looking at his face. I love his face.

I grab his hand and he holds mine as we drive over eighty miles-per-hour on the golden interstate. After a while, though, Ryker slows and merges off of the road and we drive past the same cornfield and lake that has a large forest of trees next to it. I stare and I swear I see a body standing under the moonlight, glistening black and silver in the water.

Rain.

Fire.

Crying.

Screaming.

Broken glass.

Alcohol.

Cigar smoke.

Ryker.

"Stop the car, Ryker," I suddenly say. It wasn't an angry, forceful statement but he listened.

"What are you doing? We need to get back home. It's not safe," he claims as I open the door.

I walk out to the beginning of the cornfield and stare. "Do you see him?" I whisper to Ryker without looking at him. He pants beside me.

"No. There is nothing there."

His voice is hesitant.

"You know something."

"Know what?"

"Who was over here nine years ago?"

"Nobody, Orchid."

"Ryker, when you were crying at the hospital, you weren't sad about the recent accident. You were sad about the old one."

"What do you want to hear?"

"Everything."

"He is here."

"I know."

"I should've done something. That was him—had to have been. I'm going to tell you because he is back and you deserve the truth. I'm sorry I haven't been truthful, Orchid."

We go back to his car and buckle in. Ryker locks our doors and we drive slowly away. The headlights cause the trees to cast eerie shadows beside us.

"Your dad was an alcoholic and he beat your mom. The night of the accident, three days after Independence Day, celebrating your birthday he was being specifically violent to you and your sister."

My heart stops. "My sister?"

"You had a twin sister, Orchid."

Strawberry blond hair floating.

Small, pale, skinny body mangled with the woman's. My mother's.

"They're in my dreams. My mom and my sister. What was her name?"

"Iris Lee." Ryker's voice is firm. I acknowledged it and I was excited yet terrified that I knew he was being serious with telling me what happened.

"Your mom was having a small get-together with me, my mom and dad, and your grandparents for you and Iris' birthday. Your dad was drinking as usual and I remember him starting to grab you while you were opening my gift. He said you and your sister were being spoiled and didn't deserve the presents. I can't remember where your grandparents were right at that exact moment—maybe went back to their house to grab more food or something—and your mom told him to stop or leave. He got angry and smacked her. My dad intervened and they both started to have a fist fight. They took it outside—where the cornfield and the lake is—and your dad shoved my dad into the lake after beating him nearly to death."

"Nobody helped your dad? Nobody tried to get my

dad off of him?" I ask with disbelief.

"Our moms couldn't, Orchid. They weren't strong enough to pull both of our dads apart. They were trying to get us away from the violence and they didn't think it would last long. They didn't think your father had the ability to kill anyone." Ryker's face is stern and his hands grip the steering wheel. I'm in shock. I wait for him to continue.

"My mom tried to get him, to pull me and your mom and you and Iris away, but your mom said to my mom to run and get help. Your mom took all three of us into the old shed that was next to the house you lived in and locked us in it. It was starting to get dark out and my mom didn't come back for a while. Your dad was out there taunting us for an hour. My mom told me a long time ago, sometime after the whole thing, that she thought she was going to die too as she snuck out to get help. She said he saw her running towards town, knowing what she was going to do, but she swears that there was a hint of remorse and acknowledgment in his dark eyes. He knew he was bad. He knew what he was doing was so fucking bad." Ryker was sobbing now. I watched his tears glitter against his cheeks. We are almost past the backroads and into the neighborhood. He wipes his face and continues.

"After a while of sitting, huddled together, we watch out of the windows and smell smoke. Your dad seemed like he was gone but it was obvious that he had started the fire. The town hosted fireworks every year during the evening for the Fourth of July, but they would last until July seventh—your birthday. The fireworks were exploding right by your guys' house behind the forest and your dad must have planned everything all along." The fireworks boom in my head. I close my eyes and remember the white firework exploding behind them and the rainbow hand grabbing me and the heat from the flames.

"Your mom went up to the window and I remember her gasping and looking at us with fear. She tried to hide it but I could see it."

I close my eyes and put my face in my hands.

Fire.

Glow.

Alcohol.

"Iris ran outside into the back of the forest screaming for my mom to come back, for help, and your mom followed her out of the back of the shed doors where your dad hit her on the back of the head with a beer bottle. Iris screamed and went over to your dad to attack him but he threw her against the ground and she rolled into the fire. I ran out of the shed with a shovel to try and hit your dad unconscious so that we could at least run and get my mom and help but he ripped the shovel out of my hands and hit your mom when she came at him. You then ran out and tried to attack him when you saw him hit your mom but he hit you with the shovel extremely hard in the face rather than the head. That's why you have a scar in the middle of your bottom lip."

"My injuries, Ryker," I exclaim. "I barely had any injuries besides my lip and my eyes."

"That's correct. That was the weirdest part of it all, Orchid—I'm not sure who's work it was, if it was a God or a crack in the universe—what *I* think caused your eyesight to disappear wasn't trauma. It was something else. It is something else. Do you understand me?" I don't answer.

"I remember looking over at your bloody face as you laid unconscious and you had your eyes open. I saw a lot of debris from the fire in the whites of your eyes. There was so much debris in them that they were grey. The green in your eyes were orange from the fire glazing off of them."

I rub my watering eyes. The memories make them burn.

"When we were kids, I remember you glowing purple."

"Purple?"

"Purple. Every time it rained, your aura was purple. Everyone could see it. No one talked about it, just like with the accident. There is something wrong with this town. We all seem to walk around and work like zombies and greet each other like robots with metal brains that pull any bad thoughts away. No one in this fucking town talks about what's important. Nobody in the fucking town lives in reality. You're strong. Everything around you is strong. The way you look at things is different. The way you move. The way you live in this town defies the pulp of gravity and problems and disasters."

"That's how I've always felt, Ryker," I cry. "I want out. And I feel different now that I can see . . . but I've always felt different."

"Yes. The eyesight and the dreams and the little turnout injuries—they are all a phenomenon," Ryker

claims. "You are a phenomenon. Your mom and Iris are phenomenons. The car accident—the way your head didn't bust into fucking pieces when it should have—whatever the fuck this phenomenon is, it's working. But it's never done anything for or to your dad."
"Something isn't right," I claim.

"That's true—not right in this town."

"I don't want to be abnormal. This stuff is abnormal but it feels normal to me—that's what scares me the most."

"You shouldn't be scared, Orchid. Don't ever be scared of what you have. There was literally no stopping your dad. The only thing that would have killed him right then would have been a shotgun. We never had access to a shotgun, and guns are only good killers if you have good aim. So then I went into the shed and grabbed you and I ran with your body in my hands, we ran through the fire, through broken glass bottles and cigar butts and the flames that grazed the lake. Your mom told me to take you and run. She knew you were going to be alive no matter what. She told me not to save her or Iris; that they were saved by love. They fought hate with their eternal love for you. They fought bad for you."

Ryker pulls into Christine's driveway. We both sit and breathe. I take everything in.

Pulling weeds.

Taunting.

Cigars.

Waiting.

Waiting for the flame to burn out.

Waiting to light a match to start another one.

"Let's check on Christine really quick and then I need to go to my grandparent's house. Bad is here."

THE SOUND OF RAIN

<u>Chapter Seventeen</u>

We pull into the driveway of my grandparent's house and I knock on the door.

This is the house you grew up in and you're knocking on the freaking door.

Grandma answers it. "Orchid," she breathes. I hug her.

"Grandma, I know everything. Where is Grandpa?"

"You know what?"

"Everything, Grandma. I know everything. The accident. Iris. Mom. Dad. I don't have time, we are in danger. Please. We need to go. But where is Grandpa?"

"Who told you?"

"Grandma!" I scream.

"We aren't in danger. I don't know what your talking about. You're acting crazy, Orchid. Grandpa is at the shop right now. He said he left something really important there while they were working on the shop addition."

"No, I'm not crazy. You're oblivious. You're absolutely oblivious." I snap. I run to the phone and dial the shop's number that is pinned on the fridge. "Orchid, calm down. We will go look for your grandpa." Ryker says.

"Grandpa said that it was needed and that he would be right back. He should be here any minute now." Grandma says.

"My father—my psycho fucking father—is in town to kill us. Do you understand me? I feel him. I've been feeling him for the last month. He hasn't been in town since Mom and Iris died and now that he is near me, my dreams—no, fucking nightmares—have been excruciating. I can feel things, Grandma, and I feel danger. You have to listen to me. I don't care how stubborn you naturally are or want to be, but you will listen to me right now or so help me Go—" My face stings.

Grandma pulls her hand back.

My face is lowered and my hair brushes against my stinging cheek. I look up slowly at her. My eyes burn, but not with tears.

"I'm done. I didn't understand at first, and now I do.

I understand why you left Iris and Mom and Ryker and I there to die. I understand now.

You're so selfish. And it's okay because you'll get yours. Goodbye."

I grab Ryker's hand and run out of the door. Ryker doesn't protest. Grandma's shrill yelling echoes in the air as we rush to the car.

"We need to go to the shop. Now."

****

I rush up to the bottom of the shop steps and stop. The building is the size of a smaller house and the outside is vintage and rusty. I look through the lightly lit window and see Grandpa kneeling underneath a desk like he's dropped something and is trying to pick it up. Ryker tries opening the door and it's locked, so he pulls out his key and unlocks it. I jog in first and go into the room Grandpa is in. He is still searching for whatever he dropped.

"Grandpa," I state.

Grandpa jumps up slightly and bumps his head. He gasps lightly and winces as he stands up and looks at me.

"Orca?" he asks.

"Hey, Grandpa. Please, we don't have much time—
we need to leave right now."

"What is wrong, Orca?"

"I can't really explain right now but we are in dan—
"

There is a hard thump at the window and we all stop.
And another. And another.

I inch closer to Grandpa. Ryker runs up to the office
window.

"That's it, I'm going out there. This is
ridiculous." I'm about to protest, but I look at him for
a moment. I look over at Grandpa.

"It *is* ridiculous."

"What is ridiculous, Orca?" Grandpa asks. He truly
doesn't know.

"Grandpa, Dad is back. He's here. And Grandma
isn't doing anything to stop it and neither are the police
officers or the town and we have to make sure Dad
doesn't come back anymore."

Another tap. He's taunting us. Each and every tap I hear, my chest burns hotter and hotter.

We all go out into the mail part of the shop and lock the office doors. I run around locking and covering all of the windows.

Ryker goes to the other end of the shop for a moment and walks out with a nine-millimeter pistol in his hands. I stare at it.

"We are safer the second round now," he smirks and creeps out of the only door that isn't locked: the main door. I tap him on the shoulder before he completely exits.

"Come right back in if there is nothing out there," I whisper. "I'm going to call Green County police rather than Oathpark. There are more of them and they'll be a helluva lot more help than our doughnut-eaters."

Ryker smiles slightly. "I promise. If nothing else, we will call them and make sure they come here and then flee."

I kiss him quickly on the cheek and close the door. I go over to Grandpa who is sitting in a booth by the shop phone and sit next to him.

"Orca, your father hasn't been in town in years,"

Grandpa states.

"Grandpa, weren't you paying attention to everything that's been going on? The photo? Officer Dean? The news?"

"I thought you knew I never pay attention to that stuff," I hold my eye-roll. I love Grandpa to death because of his innocence, but *really*?

"Dad hit Ryker's car," I explain. "He has been taunting this whole town. I'm not sure why he's back all of a sudden, but I'm assuming it's for me. He keeps trying to hurt us, Grandpa."

"Your grandmother—we need to get her," Grandpa claims.

"I've tried, Grandpa. I've tried." I say, starting to tear up. I can't cry now. I won't.

I blink back my stressed tears and grip the phone. I call Green County police station and they pick up after two rings.

"Hi, my name is Orchid and I'm located in Oathpark," I say, disregarding the dispatcher's greeting completely. "We really need help, please, and the phone won't connect to Oathpark's Police Station," I lie. They probably caught that lie right away but they agree and state they will be there in less than ten minutes.

"Please hurr—"

A gunshot rings in my ears and the flames that are burning the surface of my world freeze.

THE SOUND OF RAIN

<u>Chapter Eighteen</u>

Grandpa and I rush outside. My heart is beating so fast in my chest, I can't tell if it even exists.

"Ryker?" I shout.

No answer.

I grab Grandpa's hand and and we walk as fast as he is able to to the car.

"Grandpa, I'm going to go grab Ryker and we are going to get the hell out of this town, okay?" I tell him as he gets in. He buckles up and looks at me sadly.

"The shop, Orca. What about the shop? Everything and everyone here? Your grandmother—my wife?"

"Grandpa, it won't be forever. Please, stay in here and I'll be back with Ryker."

I close the car door and I have him lock it. I run towards the front of the shop and grab a metal pole about the size of my leg and make my way towards the back of the shop where I heard the gunshot.

"Ryker?" I shout.

I jog towards the shed. The light from the shop fades and I can barely see. I curse myself for not bringing a flashlight.

"Ryk—"

I bump into something hard and grunt when I hit the ground. The air is knocked out of my lungs and I'm shaking for oxygen. I back up on my hands and push myself with my legs and look up and around at the dark sky.

"Ryker?" I whisper. Nothing.

Sour alcohol and soap invades my nose.

"Dad?" I croak hesitantly, not wanting to believe he was here. The word burns my throat.

I hear him take something out of his pocket. A metal click and a hiss lights his face up as he lights his cigar. He looks just like the photo James showed me. A dark shadow of beard scruff lines his jaw and it shines gray in the flame light.

"Hi there, Orchid Blossom. Orchid Jane." I stare at him.

"Long time, no see," he takes a long drag of his cigar. "You look just like your mother."

I stand up slowly, watching his every move. "Where is Ryker?"

"Don't worry. He's roaming around here somewhere." he smirks. He takes another drag.

I walk slowly up to him and look him in his eyes. They're green.

"I'm going to ask you one more fucking time," I whisper angrily. "Where is Ryker?"

"Not sure. I heard a gunshot, though. How is that old lady of yours? Pops? They're going to be dying pretty soon, aren't they?"

I rip the cigar out of his mouth and crush it with my foot. I try to shove the metal pole into him to knock him onto the ground but he grips it and shoves me back. I'm on my butt again.

"You're a little bitch just like your mom, just like your whole family," he sneers. He leans on the pole like a walking stick.

"Good," I scream up at him. "Good. We're bitches. We aren't pieces of shit like you."

"I can feel you. I know you can feel me, Orchid." "I don't feel anything," I spit.

"You don't have to lie to me. We are the same, and that's why I'm here for you."

"You're out of luck. I'm not going anywhere with you."

"Listen to me," he says slowly, like I'm an idiot. "Our powers are the same. If you want to call them powers— our feelings—they're the same. We are the same." "I'm nothing like you," I say. "The only reason why I'm like this is because of you. You ruined me. You killed my mother and my sister. You should be in prison right now.

You don't deserve to live, and you don't deserve to die. You deserve to rot with nothing."

"No, no, see, that is where your wrong," he chuckles. His teeth are yellowed from smoking. "You've always been like this. Before whatever tragedy you'd like to call it.

When you were a snot-nosed baby, you'd cry right before it rained. You'd scream at the sky and the way your eyes glossed over when there was a tragedy playing out on the news. Your lips would purse at the slight crunch of a footstep behind you."

My eyes tear up, not believing his words. "You

killed my family," I whisper. "Why'd you do it? You killed your own family!"

"You were going to kill them eventually," he claims. "I did you a favor."

"You're the biggest liar and psychopath on this planet!" I scream.

"No, no. I think I'm pretty clever. We both glowed on the night they died. I was going to kill you, too, but I wanted to make sure they were at peace first. Your little boyfriend saved you real good." his voice has a faded Southern accent. It makes me cringe.

"What do you mean that I was going to kill them? I wasn't going to kill anybody. I was seven." I wipe my face. My legs are hurting. Where is Ryker?

"Everything about you," he inches closer. "Your whole being. You were going to kill all of us. I'm taking you with me so noth—"

"Like hell you will," Ryker's voice echoes against the night sky. I hear a gun cock.

"Ryker Feldspar. You're grown."

"Get out of here. The police are on their way." Ryker grabs my arm and pulls me away from Dad. I don't know why I keep calling him Dad. He isn't my dad at all.

"Orchid, come with me. You will always be at ease. Those dreams you have—they'll stop."

I shake my head and grab Ryker's arm. "No. I'm not going anywhere. Not with you." Danny's eyes pierce mine and my head instantly hurts. Flashes of static and screams fill my head like a tank of boiling acid waiting to spill over.

"The abuse," I snap. "I have forgotten a lot of things, but I'll never forget the abuse."

Danny smirks.

I hear slow footsteps behind me. Ryker and I both turn around.

"Orca?" Grandpa asks.

"Grandpa," I gasp. "Get back in the car, now. We will be there in a minute."

Grandpa walks a little closer. The moonlight is so bright it lights all of our faces up.

"Danny?" Grandpa asks. His face is scrunched up.

"Hey, Pops." Dad smirks.

Ryker aims his gun at Dad. "You son of a bitch, get out of here. Get out of here right now before I blow your head off."

"I don't think that'll be necessary." Danny takes the pole and walks up to us slowly.

"What the fuck did I just say?" Ryker screams. "If you don—"

Danny wacks the gun out of Ryker's hand with the metal pole and I lean into Grandpa. I steer him back to go towards the car.

"Grandpa, go right now, we will take care of this," I exclaim.

"Danny, you better knock all of this off right now," Grandpa yells at Dad. His Southern accent is deep and his yelling voice is airy. I've never heard him yell before. "What will you do?" Danny asks as he sways slightly on the pole. Ryker clenches his fists.

"You son of a *bitch*!" Ryker lunges at him as he sways and they both fall to the ground. The gun lays at least thirty feet away from us. I go to get the gun but

Danny's hand grabs my ankle and I trip. I bang my nose against the dirt ground and I hear a *crack*.

I cover my nose with my hand, which is now full of a warm, sticky liquid, and push myself over to them. Ryker is struggling to get on top but he whips his leg over Danny and pulls himself up on top of him and pins his shoulders.

"You had so many fucking chances. There are none left." Ryker snaps.

"I have plenty." Danny kicks Ryker in the groin and pushes him over. I lunge at Danny and land on top of his legs. I reach my hand up and punch him in his groin and he kicks me in my side. I shout in pain but I manage to grip his hand as he tries to get up. He shoves me away and runs over to the gun.

Ryker gets up with a groan and slightly jogs over to him, but Danny stands back up with the gun and points it at him. Ryker puts his hands up.

I jog over to them and put mine up too when Danny points it at me.

"Alright, you win." I pant.

"That's damned right." Danny says.

"You've ruined our lives enough," Ryker states.

"Enough is enough. Right now is enough. Put the fucking gun down."

"I don't think I'll be doing that anytime soon. I'll be taking all of you down, one by one, though."

"Put the gun down, Danny," Grandpa's forceful voice says behind us.

Danny ignores Grandpa completely and points the gun back at Ryker. "You're first, pretty boy."

"No!" I scream as he pulls the trigger that is aimed at Ryker's chest.

I don't realize it, but I'm toppled over with Ryker next to me. I'm shaking so hard and it hurts to breath. I push Ryker over on the ground and there is nothing on him.

He is okay.

"Orchid. . . ," Ryker sobs. His face has blood on it. His eyes are filled with tears. He looks behind me.

I slowly turn my head and Grandpa is laying on the ground, his back towards us.

I crawl over to him and pull him towards me gently. His stomach is gushing blood. It glistens in the moonlight. Hot tears sting my eyes.

"Grandpa," I sob. I cover my mouth and nose with my hand. The iron smell of his blood makes my stomach churn. I turn my head away from him and vomit.

"Orca," Grandpa breathes next to me.

I wipe my mouth. "Grandpa, it's okay, you'll be okay," I'm sobbing so hard the sentence barely comes out. I take my shirt off and put it over his stomach. My bra is soaked with sweat and my bare skin is cold.

"My Orca, everything will be okay," he whispers. "Always remember that everything is okay." I bend over him and he touches my hair.

"I'm so sorry Grandpa," I whisper. He touches my face and neck and I kiss his hand. He lays it on my shoulder and it goes limp. I lean against him and I'm crying so hard, my heart and lungs feel like they're collapsing. I clutch Grandpa's hand and put it up to my face as I cry. I hum *I Overlooked an Orchid* into his palm lightly.

As I'm holding him, Ryker's voice pierces my ears.

"You piece of *shit*!" Ryker screams. He wipes his

face and his tears and sweat glisten on his cheeks. He's holding the gun and aiming it at Danny.

Tears blur my eyes and my head is pounding so hard that I barely hear the six bullets shoot through Danny's heart.

THE SOUND OF RAIN

<u>Chapter Nineteen</u>

There are sirens everywhere.

I stare at the moon. Grandma shakes my shoulders but the moonlight blocks her face.

HANA FERGUSON

My nose hurts.

THE SOUND OF RAIN

<u>Chapter Twenty</u>

Less Than a Week Later

I spend my birthday alone today.

Christine is at work now but we had a small party together last night. And by party, I mean she forced me to decorate a cake with her and watch movies and eat food.

I just wanted to stay in bed. It's been almost a week since Grandpa died and since Ryker got taken away.

Grandpa's funeral is tomorrow.

Ryker's court-date is the day after tomorrow.

I grab a piece of leftover cake out of the fridge and stick a small, thin candle in it. I light the candle and watch the small flame build up and glow. A quick flash of fire and smoke and water appear behind my eyes. I don't react to it. Instead, I sit still and continue to pick at my cake. The cold frosting forms small water droplets on it because of the humidity and heat. The flame still burns.

I blow the candle out and chuck the cake into the

trashcan by the garage. It tips over. I leave it there and fall asleep on the porch bench swing.

HANA FERGUSON

My heart hurts.

I Overlooked an Orchid is on repeat in my head.

HANA FERGUSON

<u>Chapter Twenty-One</u>

Four Months Later - Christmas Eve

The broken zipper on my jacket and the thorns of a red rose scratches the palm of my hand as I walk.

Cold water sprinkles above me and I put my hood up. My camera hangs around my neck and I put it underneath my shirt so it doesn't get wet. I open the raggedy umbrella that I haven't touched in months and I yearn for Ryker's hand against mine.

I'm going to put a rose on Grandpa's grave. It's Christmas Eve and Decembers in Florida are nothing but chilly. No snow, no beautiful white landscapes like I see in movies. We go from barely wearing anything to wearing a jacket. It doesn't rain much here in December, but oddly enough, it's raining today. The grass underneath me is starting to get soggy and all of the cement graves are stained with water droplets and have milky charcoal cracks in them—all but Grandpa's. His grave is too fresh.

The total amount of graves in Oathpark's

cemetery is eighteen.

I go over to his grave that has a weeping willow tree that hangs down over it like green strands of hair. I sit and lean against it, the droopy strands blocking some of the waterfall. I set the dewy rose on the flat part of his gravestone and switch the umbrella into my other hand. I sit in silence with my eyes closed.

The flashbacks have stopped. The dreams have subsided for the most part. Once in awhile, Iris will appear in my dreams for a split second but nothing happens—it's simply Iris. Mom doesn't show up in my dreams anymore.

I still feel things. I feel everything around me, like the universe is planted into my veins. I see things still, too, and *not* in a crazy way. I go to school and work at a clinic outside of Oathpark part-time. I saw Maria stop in once a month or so ago, and she still looks the same. She hugged me and I haven't seen her since.

The best part about having a job now is I make my own money and I bought the camera that hangs around my neck. It's the first time I've ever been involved with something outside of Oathpark besides The Rolling Stones concert, and I can sometimes see a patient's wound in colors. I've studied chakras and I think that is what I see, but I'm still unsure. I'm interested in the medical profession and I might do something after I graduate high school. I also really like photography and capturing the whole world around me. It's a new life.

I've tried telling Claire and Beth, the women I work with, about seeing the patients and their colorful wounds, but they don't really listen. I just organize paperwork and keep my mouth shut. That portion is the same, until I'm able to leave Oathpark for good. I dream about leaving every night. Dreaming makes my brain turn to mush.

I've never figured out why my sight came back. Cliché as it sounds, it was an act that God played rather than me playing him. God has played me a lot throughout my life; my choice is whether or not I choose to play life as it goes on.

Danny's true intentions weren't exactly clear. Obviously he wanted to kill me, but I never figured out everything he said. What he said about how we were alike—I'll never truly know. Maybe this whole phenomenon, the way I feel things, the way he felt things, was what he meant. What Ryker meant. I choose to block it out and move on.

I still don't have many friends besides Ryker. I talk to Jewel and James and we go on picnics sometimes and listen to music at each other's houses. It's hard to do so without Ryker, though.

It's been four months since the court trial. Ryker wasn't convicted of anything because he killed Danny in self-defense; but he was sent to a juvenile detention center in Green County. Christine had agreed to let him go because she thought it'd help him 'heal from this town.' I argued and argued and argued with her, but he agreed to go, too. I didn't talk to Christine *or* Ryker for two weeks. I was furious because my grandfather had just died and they were taking away another person I loved the most. I gave in though when Ryker sent me twenty-two letters over the course of those two weeks. We wrote each other back and forth at least three times a week after that. A letter Ryker wrote me consisted of childhood memories that I don't remember but that I still had a weird feeling for, like I knew that we experienced everything together. He told me more things about my father and his connections. He told me that it's okay to move on now; that it's always okay to move on. He also told me how much the food sucks there and that he misses Daisy Doughnuts.

Today is the day he gets out of Green County's

juvenile facility. I was going to bring his Christmas present today, but I feel like he would want to wait until tomorrow morning. I check my wrist watch and I'm suppose to be meeting him at the bus station in an hour.

I still live with Christine and I sometimes help her with her accountant work, but I'm not super great at math. She works today and she wanted to be here to meet Ryker at the bus station, but she wasn't able to take the day off. I talk to my grandma once in awhile. We don't get along still but I visit her. She has a broken heart and isn't the same. She sits in Grandpa's chair most of the day and watches television. I got her into a doctor when she was worse but she takes medication now and she isn't that bad anymore. She took all of the pictures off of the shelf in the living room.

I start to get up and I feel something skitter against the top of my hand. I pull my hand away and gasp. A white mouse sits right next to the rose.

I look closely at it and its eyes glisten. I smile lightly and reach my finger out slowly to touch it and it watches me. I poke its ear lightly and it scurries behind the gravestone. I sigh, stand up, and pat Grandpa's gravestone one last time. I look back over at the mouse and it sits quietly behind Grandpa's grave still. I pull my camera out slowly and snap a picture of the mouse. I start to walk off and the mouse watches me.

The rain is cold but it still comforts me. I feel it wash away all the bad I've possessed. It washes away some of my sorrow and purifies my new intentions. Somehow, it drips and patches up everything that needs to be fixed.

I shove the camera back into my shirt and make my way to the small bus station, which is right next to Oathpark's townhouse, and when I get there, I close the umbrella and sit on an enclosed bus bench. Faint Christmas music echos against the hollow walls of the bus station and colorful Christmas lights decorate small bushes and trees in pots. They twinkle against the raindrops. I check my wrist watch again and I'm over half an hour early. The rain is pouring down harder now and I'm thankful I'm sitting under some sort of covering. A young black woman sits next to me and pulls out a magazine.

"It'll be awhile, baby," she says without looking up at me.

"That's okay. It's something worth waiting for."

She smiles. "Definitely something worth waiting for if you're waiting in this damned rain."

I laugh. "Yeah. My boyfriend is getting out of jail today."

I'm afraid she's going to ask me about what happened or question me if I'm 'that one girl that was blind' like everyone else, but she just looks up at me with a small smile and her eyebrows raised. Her eyes are big and brown and her eyelashes are dark and curled. "Early Christmas present, huh?" I smile and nod.

"Always remember this, honey: everything will always turn out okay in the end. I'm glad he has a new beginning. You seem like you do, too." I pick at my nails and look back up at her.
"Everything will be okay," I agree.

She looks at my shirt. "What is that bulge in your chest?"

I look at her with wide, questioning eyes, but then I realize she's talking about my camera. "I'm carrying my camera."

"Are you a photographer?"

I shake my head no. "I like seeing the world through a different lens."

I like seeing the world without forgetting it.

"Very nice. You can take my picture if you want some practice." she poses and smiles with her magazine.

I laugh and pull my camera out. "Okay, in one . . . two . . . three," *Click.* "Beautiful."

She smiles and goes back to her magazine. A few minutes later, a young black man greets her and they hug. She gets up and says goodbye to me. I wish her a Merry Christmas.

For the next half hour, I watch people come and go alone on the bench. Some are wearing work clothes and suits, others are wearing sweatpants. I wonder what they're doing for Christmas.

I remember one year for Christmas when I was blind, Grandpa let me decorate the Christmas tree all by myself. I was nine and I thought that that was the greatest perk of being an adult: to be able to buy and decorate a tree for Christmas. I couldn't wait to be an adult. I decorated it and as I did, I went by how the branches felt and which ornament string would sit the best on each branch. The smell of pine stung my nose and the small bulbs from the Christmas lights were warm against my fingertips.

When I was done, I nearly fell off of the chair getting down. Grandpa helped me down and he stood behind me in silence for a few long moments. He placed both of his hands on my shoulders. I could hear the smile in his voice.

"Orca, you did a very good job," he said. "Do you remember how many ornaments you placed up there?"

"I wasn't counting," I stated.

"There are a lot, but each of them line up with each other like a swirl. A perfect swirl, I tell you."

I smiled wide, my missing front tooth showing and everything, and go up to the tree to feel it.

The ornaments bumped against my fingers indeed in a straight swirl as I brushed my hand against them to feel their order. They were in a perfect swirl.

I'm leaning back on the bench with my eyes closed, listening to the beat of the raindrops against the top of the bench covering, when I hear a grunt next to me. I open my eyes and Officer Dean is holding two Styrofoam cups filled with a warm, brown liquid. It steams up into the chilly rainy air.

"I knew you'd be here. Hot chocolate?"

I give him a small, tight smile and take the cup

from him. I blow on it lightly, holding the cup with my hands that are wrapped in my jacket sleeves.

"You were right. I never did anything. This town is under something, something I can't put my finger on, and I'm trying to get over it," he says, his words genuine. I look over at him with interest. "I'm sorry."

"It's okay. It's not your fault. I never really said anything to anyone. I was a spoiled bitch. I felt things and knew things and I did nothing. That 'something' feels kind of like a cloud, huh?"

"A cloud, indeed. I think the sun is finally starting to shine through it, though. At least until this shitty rain stops."

I laugh. "Yeah. Rain has a lot of different meanings," I look at the sky and thin light beams land on the grass across the street. "There should be a rainbow but I don't see it."

"Rain washes old things away and makes new things grow," he agrees. "It can mean sadness, happiness, and love. A rainbow will be across the street behind the bus, the way the light is shining."

I watch. The sun is still faint but bright.

"If it makes you feel better, your grandpa would

be very proud of you."

I smile and nod. "I think he would, too. Of all of us."

"This town is moving on to something better. Oathpark Police is entirely new. I'm not the only chief there anymore, and it feels pretty damn good." he takes a sip of his hot chocolate and I do the same. It's warm and sweet.

"Please keep an eye on Grandma for me," I say. "I'm going to travel the world and take pictures one day and I can't always be here. I know she will stay."

"Promise." he says. He takes his coat off and puts it around my shoulders and I don't protest.

"Merry Christmas, Officer Dean."

"Merry Christmas, Orchid."

We sit in silence for a while as I drink the rest of my hot chocolate. I hear screeching tires and a hot *sizzle* and look up. The bus sits across the street and it has rust on it. It drips with water and rainbow oil. I stand up and shove my hands in Officer Dean's coat pockets nervously as I watch people trudge off of the bus and struggle to open their umbrellas right away. Officer Dean sits and watches.

I look around the station quickly so I don't look like I'm anxiously waiting and there are patches of graffiti stamped onto some of the brick walls that line the small station. There is a saying that says in big, bold, blue letters with soft ocean waves speckled with green and yellow: "*Float in the ocean we call life—drowning isn't an option.*" I whip my camera out and take a photo.

"Orchid Jane," Officer Dean says behind me.

I turn around.

"Remember that Oathpark is just a lake. This world is your entire ocean."

He gets up and starts to walk off into the rain without looking back.

I look past the cheesiness of his saying and agree with it in my head.

I look back over at the bus and a sudden brightness shocks my eyes. I cover them for a moment and look back up slowly. The rain is still pouring down, but the sun has finally creeped out to its full potential.

The water droplets glitter in the sun as they fall and splash into sparkling puddles.

THE SOUND OF RAIN

A boy with shaggy brown hair and a pair of jeans and a grey T-shirt stands in front of the bus. I brought him a pair of clothes last week knowing he was getting out today. His T-shirt gets darker with every drop of rain pouring down and it soaks his hair. His damp skin glistens in the sun.

The bus screeches and drives off. Behind him, a half-circular strip of colors fading at the ends floats.

I have forgotten a lot of things, but I will not forget this.

He lifts up a hand and waves. He smiles.

I smile until my cheeks hurt and pull out my camera. I take a picture of him and the rainbow.

I get the picture of life and everything is finally clear.

I have forgotten a lot of things, but I will not forget. . . ,

HANA FERGUSON

. . . there is nothing between us but *the sound of rain.*

HANA FERGUSON

ACKNOWLEDGEMENTS

For the readers who have reached this part of my book: thank you from the bottom of my heart. I worked extremely hard under pressure; and you know the saying: diamonds are made under pressure, so there ya go. Hopefully this book is a diamond to you—just not as expensive.

Thank you to everyone who supported me on this journey with my first novel: Tanner, Aunt Tracy, Mom and Dad, the rest of my family, my wonderful editor and friend Isabela Mendes, my other friend, Cecilia Schmitt, who created a great novel cover, and all of my additional wonderful friends who have supported me through thick and thin: Andrew Fadness, Erin Davis, Cassidy Poden, Elizabeth Stormont, and JoJo. I'd also like to thank additional editors and supporters: Emily Knipp, a great friend who helped me edit, Tiffany Rochelle, a family friend and author of *Insane Roots - A Memoir: The Adventures of a Con-Artist and Her Daughter*, who also edited for me, my cousin whom I look up to dearly, Mandy Nicosia, who is just as creative and spontaneous, as well as Jeff Myerson who has supported my writing since day one and has critiqued me to my best.

A very special thank you to all of the members from my high school Writer's Club---you all have a special place in my heart, for you all as a group have helped me grow out of my shell to share the things we are most afraid of sharing.

Thank you to the Rockford Writer's Guild, as I wouldn't have grown as a writer and as a person without you all. Thank you for teaching me the values of writing, for teaching and showing me how to write, and to always appreciate my writing even if I sometimes think it's the worst idea thought of.

And, a *huge* (*HUGE!!!*) thank you to my art teacher who has taught me not only art lessons, but life lessons throughout my high school career: Mrs. V. Thank you for teaching me to always push myself to my fullest potential and to create things even when I think I can't create anymore, not only in every single art class I have had with you, but in life; for life should be full of art and writing and the beautiful things we take in to escape the uncreative eye of this rusty, mechanical pupil called society.

My love for old music and the natural aspects of how we sense things on Earth may or may not connect with everyone, but I hope this novel makes you feel something. There is one thing I have learned throughout my passion for creating things: music, art, and writing should make you feel things. If it doesn't, it isn't created to its full potential yet.

Here is the playlist of songs on my Spotify account that inspired The Sound of Rain. Some are actually featured in the book and some simply inspired it. In no particular order:

1. Free Fallin' - Tom Petty
2. Yellow - Coldplay
3. Rhiannon - Fleetwood Mac
4. Have You Ever Seen The Rain? - Creedence Clearwater Revival
5. Gimme Shelter - The Rolling Stones
6. Edge of Seventeen - Stevie Nicks
7. Iris - Goo Goo Dolls
8. Free Bird - Lynyrd Skynyrd
9. Paint It, Black - The Rolling Stones
10. Kiss - Prince
11. Under The Bridge - Red Hot Chili Peppers
12. No Diggity - Blackstreet, Dr. Dre, & Queen Pen
13. Scar Tissue - Red Hot Chili Peppers
14. Torn - Natalie Imbruglia
15. Wonderwall - Oasis
16. Champagne Supernova - Oasis
17. Shine - Collective Soul
18. All The Small Things - blink-182
19. If You Could Only See - Tonic
20. Crazy - Aerosmith
21. Hold Out Your Hand - Nickelback
22. Say It Ain't So - Weezer
23. 1979 - Smashing Pumpkins
24. Kiss Me - Sixpence None The Richer

25. Wildflowers - Tom Petty
26. Breakdown - Tom Petty and The Heartbreakers
27. November Rain - Guns N' Roses
28. Walk A Thin Line - Fleetwood Mac
29. Gold Dust Woman - Fleetwood Mac
30. Gypsy - Fleetwood Mac
31. When You're Gone - The Cranberries
32. Your Song - Elton John
33. Meet Virginia - Train
34. How's It Going To Be - Third Eye Blind
35. Fortunate Son - Creedence Clearwater Revival

For more information on the playlist, go to www.Spotify.com and look up "The Sound of Rain *Book Playlist*" or my name, "Hana Ferguson".

-Much love,
    Hana Ferguson